Readers love the Bird Face

Cynthia Toney has written anoth.. .... friendship and the complicated issues that many teens face, this one with the beautiful messages of encouraging teens to share their troubles with their parents and offering kindness even to the unkind.

Wendy is such an admirable character in the way she longs to bring comfort and joy to her elderly friend who has Alzheimer's. She is a three-dimensional character with interests in writing, sign language, and cute little wolf pups, but she also has room to grow. The more she tries to help her friends in this story, the more of a mess she makes! This is especially true of her relationship with Dev—a girl with many secrets. Wendy becomes so suspicious of Dev's motives that she even starts to lose faith in her best friend, Sam. Her stepsister gives her great advice that we can all benefit from: "There's always more to a person's story than you think when you first meet them."

With a beautiful Alaskan setting, mystery, and drama, teen readers are sure to love this fourth book in The Bird Face Series. If they've read the first three books, like I have, they will also enjoy revisiting favorite characters. Ever since reading *6 Dates to Disaster*, I've been looking forward to finding out more about Sam, and this story does not disappoint."

~**Theresa Linden**
author of award-winning
Catholic teen fiction

Cynthia T. Toney's writing is such a breath of fresh air and reminds me of enjoying a glass of lemonade on beautiful summer day. Refreshing, sweet, and delightful.

3 Things to Forget is the beautiful conclusion to Cynthia T. Toney's heart-warming *Bird Face* series. To witness Wendy grow in her faith and mature into a lovely young lady through this series has been wonderful. What a treat it has been to follow Wendy on her journey through middle school and into high school. This character has faced many obstacles with exuberance, determination, kindness, and a strong faith. I think there are many positive lessons for young people throughout these books.

I especially love how the author brings unique characters and interests to all her stories. In this series, readers can easily relate to issues many students face but are also introduced to things they might not know as much about such as - Cajun-Americans, Alzheimer's, American sign-language, Jewish culture, blended families, and animal rescue organizations. Toney's writing is full of wonderful discussion opportunities to explore.

So, relax, pour a delicious glass of lemonade, and treat yourself to *3 Things to Forget*.

Leslea Wahl
author of award-winning YA novels,
The Perfect Blindside* and *An Unexpected Role

3 Things
to Forget

by Cynthia T. Toney

W

3 Things to Forget
© 2018 Cynthia T. Toney
ISBN: 978-1-944120-62-7

This book is a work of fiction. Names, characters, places, and incidents are either products of the author's imagination or used fictitiously. Any similarity to actual people and/or events is purely coincidental.

Published by:

 Write Integrity Press
PO Box 702852
Dallas, TX 75370

Contact the author at birdfacewendy@gmail.com or www.cynthiattoney.com
www.WriteIntegrity.com

Printed in the United States of America.

Contents

Dedication

To teens everywhere.
May you make the most of
where God leads you.

Chapter 1

There's something to be said for escaping 4500 miles to the third least-populated state in America, where no one (well, almost no one) knows me. Otherwise, leaving behind my disgrace from the biggest academic scandal ever to hit my school—resulting in the breakup with my boyfriend on the night he said he loved me—might've been impossible.

Surrounded by strangers on the second of two connecting flights to Anchorage, for a total of fourteen hours on a Friday, I summoned teeth-grinding determination to forget the past. What better time for an intense study, a.k.a. cramming, of American Sign Language? Before the plane would land in Alaska, I might become proficient enough in ASL to communicate with Sam and his deaf friends without making a fool of myself. For six weeks starting in June, I would live with Sam and his family in Anchorage. I'd work with him and other teens, possibly deaf, as a volunteer at the Alaska

Wildlife Conservation Center. And I'd do whatever it took to fit in.

The glossy title page of my new ASL instruction book glinted under the cabin's overhead lights, ink and paper providing an odor preferable to the cabin's stale, recycled air.

The ASL book was a post-breakup, going-away gift from ex-boyfriend, David Griffin. Like David had asked, I'd waited and unwrapped the package after I boarded the first plane, the one that took me from New Orleans to Seattle. David had written inside the cover: *To Wendy. Always, David.*

His sweet face appeared once again in my mind's eye, the way he'd looked that day on the school lawn when he presented his gift. His curly brown hair and incredible green eyes had nearly killed me.

I sniffed and swallowed back tears.

This faraway trip would be just what I needed to get over the pain of being forced by David's parents to stop seeing each other.

Or it might make me miss him even more.

Sigh. At this point, how could I tell what I'd feel once I didn't see him every day at school and couldn't accidentally bump into him at church or in town?

I could only hope Mr. and Mrs. Griffin would eventually recognize my conduct that had turned them against me as an honest—though stupid—mistake.

Ugh. My mind always wandered back to those final

weeks of school. This trip was supposed to help me forget all that. *Focus on learning ASL.*

As I had on the first leg of the trip, I turned again to the page that featured the ASL alphabet. After a quick review of the individual letters, I flipped to the pages of whole-word signs. Following the illustrations, I struggled to imitate the hand shapes and movements. I'd have to be able to fingerspell some basic personal information, but I'd also need to know numbers and common whole-word signs. There was so much I wanted to learn and practice. I'd gotten by in communicating with Sam when I met him because he could read my lips pretty well. But Sam's friends might ask me for my age, where I live, and where I go to school. Why did *Louisiana* have to be such a long word?

A college-age guy across the aisle from me stared at my awkward, jerky hand movements. I made eye contact. He reclined his seat and closed his eyes.

Soon I grew tired and closed the book, resting it on my lap with the fingers of one hand curled around the edge. I would try again after a break. Where was that beverage cart?

I looked at my watch. Only a few more hours and I'd be in Anchorage. As eager as I was to see Sam again, I couldn't wait to see Mrs. V. I missed her terribly since she moved to Anchorage to live near Sam's family because of her Alzheimer's. It was like she was my own grandmother as much as Sam's. As I recalled my eight years with Mrs. V, my eyelids grew heavy. I relaxed my grip on the book.

Next thing I knew, I awoke to an announcement that the plane was approaching Anchorage.

I blinked my eyes several times. I needed eye drops… and a breath mint. *Yuck.* A lot of breath mints.

The book lay at my feet. I picked it up, along with my tote bag. One glimpse through the window at snow-laced mountains, and I slung the cardigan over my shoulders that Mom had insisted I carry on the flight.

My phone pinged. A text from Sam.

WE JUST PARKED. MEET YOU IN BAGGAGE CLAIM.

My skin tingled. Could Mrs. V be included in that "we"? Was she well enough to come to the airport with Sam? When she left Louisiana last fall, she didn't seem to understand what was happening to her, much less remember our relationship.

Eyes and breath refreshed, legs stiff and wobbly, I left the plane and followed the terminal's signs. I arrived in baggage claim and located my flight's carousel. Waiting for my single piece of blue luggage to show up, I glanced occasionally at the door for Sam and whoever might be with him.

"Wendy."

His voice had deepened over the past nine months but still had the nasally sound of someone who'd been deaf since early childhood.

Smiling, I turned and signed, "Hi." Totally

10

unnecessary, but I was eager to show off my new skill.

"Impressive. What else do you know?" The happiness in the lift of his broad mouth reached to his light golden-brown eyes, and they twinkled. Sun eyes, I used to call them.

I didn't have a chance to answer Sam with any of the other signs I'd learned. His father and a woman I guessed to be his mother, along with an older version of little Sarah from Mrs. V's photo albums, surrounded Sam and me.

No Mrs. V appeared, but I reined in my disappointment.

"Hi, Mr. Villaturo," I said to Sam's father. He towered over me like a brown giant, his size intimidating me like it had in Louisiana.

He signed as he spoke.

"Hello, Wendy. Please call me Tony." He smiled, and the tension in my shoulders relaxed. "This is my wife, Theresa, and Sam's sister, Sarah."

Sam's mother and sister had blonde hair like Sam's. Sarah's timid smile reminded me of my Cajun cousin Mattie, both about twelve years old and shy.

"It's nice to meet you both." I didn't really feel comfortable calling adults by their first names, at least not to their faces. Southerners like me usually added "Mr." or "Miss" to the first name when addressing an adult, whether the person was married or not. One month in Alaska wouldn't change almost fifteen years of living in the South.

"We're so happy you could come." Miss Theresa hugged me and grinned with the same broad mouth as Sam's.

"Me too. Thank you for making it possible." Being there was a dream come true. Mr. Tony had surprised me by mailing a check to cover my flight so I could visit Mrs. V. He'd said she missed me and needed me. That was after I had to pay back my classmates all the money I'd earned tutoring them. Well, tutoring was a relative word.

So, where was Mrs. V? I prayed her Alzheimer's hadn't worsened so much that she was confined to the nursing home where she lived.

Afraid to ask about her, I focused on the luggage carousel. The crowd around it had dwindled, and few bags remained.

"There's my bag, the blue one." I pointed and signed "blue."

"I'll get it." Sam's long legs reached it in three steps.

He carried the bag for me as we walked to the parking garage.

With everyone settled in the Villaturos' car, Mr. Tony spoke from behind the wheel. "Wendy, are you hungry or thirsty? We could drive through someplace."

"Not really hungry, but I could use a milkshake or ice cream for energy."

"That sounds good." Sam's mom turned toward the back seat and signed "ice cream" to Sam. Her hand

12

movement looked like an ice cream cone being licked.

Everyone smiled. Sarah, seated in the back between Sam and me took my hand.

I liked her already.

Should I ask about Mrs. V? What if I spoiled the mood? But if I didn't ask, they might think I didn't care.

Before my lips could part, Miss Theresa turned her head toward me over the back of her seat. "Wendy, we thought you'd be too tired tonight, but tomorrow I can take you to see Ana. Is that what you call her?"

"I call her Mrs. V. Thank you. I'd love that."

Sam's eyebrows pushed together like he didn't catch the whole conversation. "Visit Grandma?"

His mom nodded and made the sign for tomorrow.

I took a deep breath. Miss Theresa didn't give a clue about how Mrs. V was doing. Neither did Sam's expression. I said a silent prayer that she'd remember me and that everything would be fine.

3 Things to Forget

Chapter 2

The next morning at Sam's house, I awoke to noise. Lots of it. Knocking into walls, slamming doors, banging sounds.

Right. Sam wouldn't know how much noise he makes.

Sarah yelled in a high pitch from the hall outside my room, "Mom, Sam's gonna wake Wendy up."

I laughed and threw back the covers. As I rolled out of bed and reached the floor, my foot struck a piece of paper. A sheet of lined school paper had been slid under my door.

Hi, Lazy. Enjoy this weekend because Monday we start volunteer work. You're a special, short-term, unskilled volunteer because you're from out of state and here only a little while. I already told them you want poop-scooping duty. Sam

Gr-r-r-r. He'd better be kidding! Where was my ASL book? To look up something to call him. Then I'd get dressed.

As I entered the kitchen, I made sure his mom wasn't watching. Opening my eyes big and nodding my head, I signed to Sam, "You, pain in the neck."

He snorted and stomped his foot.

Miss Theresa turned toward the sound and spotted me. "Good morning, Wendy. How do you like your eggs?"

"However you make them for Sam or Sarah is fine with me."

"Scrambled it is, then. Would you mind putting two more slices of bread in the toaster?"

"Glad to." I turned toward Sam and had to fingerspell "lazy" but then signed "boy."

That got him laughing out loud.

Talking to Sam like this would be fun, especially if I could learn more whole-word signs to communicate faster.

I followed Sam and Miss Theresa through the doors of The Haven, Mrs. V's assisted living residence. Mr. Tony and Sarah had stayed behind for Sarah's gymnastics lesson.

Frail-looking elderly ladies and men sat in wheelchairs in the lobby or moved through it as caregivers pushed them to other destinations. A few of the residents' heads drooped to their chests. Some of the senior citizens used walkers, their steps slow and careful. The sight of them crushed my heart, and I could've wrapped my arms around each one of them. If Mrs. V had deteriorated to their condition, I was going to cry for sure when I saw her.

"Is Mrs. V in a wheelchair?" I whispered to Miss Theresa.

She kept her voice low. "So far, only for short periods. Depends on how her medications affect her." She did some signing to Sam that I didn't understand.

I fingered the silver puppy charm in my pocket, tied with a red ribbon that could slip onto my wrist like a bracelet. Mrs. V had given the charm to me after she'd been diagnosed with Alzheimer's but while she still seemed like herself. When I helped her get ready to leave Louisiana, she didn't seem to remember me. But she must've remembered a lot later. Enough so that Mr. Tony sent for me. Maybe the charm would spark her memory of our friendship.

Sam tapped my arm. "What's in your pocket?"

I withdrew the charm and pointed to my wrist.

"Put it on," he said.

I slipped it over my hand, and he smiled like he knew it had come from Mrs. V. Maybe he'd helped her select my gift. I hadn't thought of that before.

Miss Theresa knocked gently on the door to Mrs. V's

apartment and signed for Sam as she spoke to me. "Alzheimer's is an unpredictable disease. We never know what to expect."

I also signed as I spoke. "I remember."

Miss Theresa released the door handle and gently pushed the door open. The air that met me had a country-floral disinfectant scent.

My eyes adjusted from the bright hallway to the soft lighting inside. We entered a kitchen and breakfast area with a tiny table and three chairs against a wall. Mrs. V sat in a small living room a few feet beyond, on the flowered sofa from her old house, staring at a television.

"Hi, Ana." Miss Theresa spoke softly. Mrs. V didn't move.

I stayed back. What if I startled her by being there?

"She's so used to caregivers coming in and going out, she sometimes doesn't look up." Miss Theresa's sad eyes crinkled at me. She sat on a hard chair close to Mrs. V and reached toward her hand.

Mrs. V noticed her, and Miss Theresa motioned for Sam to come closer.

"Hi, Grandma." Sam used a voice not so loud as the one he used with me, as though he knew he needed to tone it down around Mrs. V. Could he tell the difference?

Mrs. V smiled, her pale lips quivering. "Hello."

Sam sat next to her.

Recognition lit Mrs. V's face. She placed a hand on his knee.

Miss Theresa rose and returned to where I stood near the door. She wrapped an arm around my shoulders and whispered, "When she recognizes us, she still sometimes has trouble remembering our names. I just wanted you to know. Ready to say 'Hi'?"

"Yes. Thank you."

I took small steps into the living room and sat in a chair opposite Mrs. V, where she could see me. Sam motioned me with his head to come to the sofa, so I moved and sat on the other side of Mrs. V from Sam.

He reached across the front of Mrs. V for my wrist, the one with the puppy charm.

Mrs. V looked down at my arm, spotted the charm, and blinked. Then she raised her eyes to my face.

"Hi, Mrs. V." My eyes filled with tears. "I've missed you."

Her face broke into a huge smile, and my heart almost burst. Sam got up and let me have her all to myself. I gently rubbed her back. We sat there together for a while, and I was glad to be next to her again on her flowered sofa.

Mrs. V didn't talk much during the rest of our visit, but she seemed to recognize me the whole time. If not exactly me, Wendy, at least me as someone familiar to her. Eyes bright and happy, she showed me things throughout her apartment. Without speaking, she handed me a Christmas card someone had mailed to her. She pointed out framed photographs of people I didn't recognize. She insisted I lift and hold delicate figurines from a shelf. Sometimes she used words that made no sense in a sentence that I guessed referred to what she was showing me. If I didn't understand, I simply nodded and smiled. She seemed satisfied with that. Being with her was enough for me.

When we sat down again in the living room, I carried a bottle of moisturizing lotion from the bathroom. Sam was helping Miss Theresa move some things around in Mrs. V's bedroom.

I rubbed lotion on my hands as Mrs. V watched me, her facial features relaxed. I extended a hand to her, and she placed one of hers in mine. She'd taken care of me years ago when I was alone while Mom was working. Now I wanted to take care of her as much as I could. I gently massaged lotion into the veined skin of her fragile hands that seemed to have shrunk since I last saw her. Just like the rest of her.

Mrs. V's attention drew back to the television.

"She's probably tired, and they'll bring her dinner soon. I think it's time for us to go," Miss Theresa whispered.

When we kissed Mrs. V goodbye, she didn't respond. We quietly walked out the door.

I trembled and rubbed my arms. It just wasn't fair. Not fair at all for this to happen to Mrs. V.

Sam must've read my face, because he gently took my hand.

I lay in bed that night staring into my room darkened with blackout shades, unable to fall asleep. No dream could've been as unreal as the past two days had been— starting with the long flight far from home to a land exciting and wild, but about as different from Louisiana as I could've imagined. Then there was Mrs. V, her new personality so unlike the energetic and talkative one I remembered before she got sick. Ten months ago, I wouldn't have believed any of it. And as much as I liked Mrs. V's family, it was strange being with them but without her.

And Monday would likely be even stranger.

3 Things to Forget

Chapter 3

The alarm went off at 5:30 Monday morning, and I awoke with a start. It took all my eye muscles to pry my lids open. What had I signed myself up for? I groaned and rolled toward the sound to turn it off.

In a second, my door boomed with what could only be a pounding from Sam's fist.

"Get up. It takes an hour to get there."

"All right," I yelled back, even though he couldn't hear me.

I opened the door to make my way to the bathroom and ran into a package at my feet. Delight filled my groggy brain. Did Sam know my birthday was coming up? Wrapped in plain white paper, a note was taped to it.

This will help you ID the animals. Sam.

Excited to open any type of gift, I ripped off the wrapping. Inside was a clear plastic bag containing a printed tee-shirt. I liked those. I withdrew and unfolded it.

Poop in the Woods, it read at the top, followed by

Who Dung It?! and was complete with pictures assigned to various animals.

I coughed out a laugh. This had to be a joke. Or a test. Sam thought I wouldn't actually put it on. I'd show him.

After my shower, I walked into the kitchen wearing the shirt over my jeans. I'd be a good sport but change before leaving.

Sam's whole family was sitting down to eat breakfast. Everyone looked up and stared. Sam wore the same shirt. It wasn't a joke.

Sarah giggled. "I didn't think you'd wear it."

Sam signed to Sarah, "You owe me," but I didn't catch the payoff.

"Sorry, Wendy. I told him it was tacky." Miss Theresa scrunched her eyes.

Tony raised his brow and met my gaze. He immediately lowered his eyes and buttered a slice of toast.

"It's okay. I can take a joke." I signed "joke" to Sam.

He shook his head and said, "No joke. We're wearing these today."

I visually sought sympathy from the rest of the family, but they avoided looking at me further and stuffed food into their mouths.

We finished breakfast, and still no one had mentioned how Sam and I would get to the Conservation Center. Everyone else left Sam and me standing in the kitchen.

"Let's go." He scooped up a set of keys from the

24

you been to the Conservation Center before?"

He nodded. "Sightseeing lots of times when I was a kid. And I took the volunteer orientation last spring. But I'll go with you and the others for a refresher today."

A volunteer coordinator welcomed us and a dozen other teenagers. Then a center tour guide took us all on the walking tour. It was a long one. The place was huge because animals lived in their natural habitats, unlike the small enclosures at most zoos, which I didn't care for. Sam and I loved the Bear Walk, where we walked a bridge high above the bear habitat and saw a climbing black bear and also some brown grizzly bears.

At the end of the tour, I stood in line in the gift shop to buy a few small souvenirs while I still had some time and money. As Sam stood with his hands in the pockets of his cargo shorts, looking up and around the shop, I had a flashback to the first time I saw him in Louisiana. He'd posed the same way while looking up into the trees at the squirrels playing in Mrs. V's yard.

Soon, he should do something out of the ordinary to indicate his newly revealed age. He should act more mature than what I'd seen from him so far. For instance, the *Poop-in-the-Woods* shirt.

Time would tell, I supposed.

Thank goodness the Conservation Center provided all us volunteers with new, matching shirts. I gladly changed out of my tee-shirt, which apparently was popular with visitors.

"They fly off the shelves," the gift-shop worker had informed us.

While some of the others seemed comfortable without a sweater or jacket, I wasn't used to cool temperatures in June and put my cardigan back on over my new shirt. Then I met Sam at the designated spot for all the volunteers to gather again. We waited with the rest of the little uniformed army for orientation to continue.

Sam and I milled about until Sam slapped an arm around another boy's shoulders. "Wendy, this is my friend Levi. He's seventeen, an old man." Sam signed as he spoke.

The boy with curly black hair and glasses grinned and signed, "Hi."

I returned the sign and a smile. My gaze drew to a silver Star of David on a chain around Levi's neck. I automatically reached for the gold crucifix hanging from my own, my inheritance from Grandma Robichaud, and then dropped my hand. My face warmed. Did he think I was making an unspoken statement about our difference?

Levi didn't miss my hand's movement, but his smile never left his lips.

I sighed with relief. We'd both acknowledged God without making an issue of the other's religion.

He signed something new, but I recognized only the first sign, "one."

I shifted my gaze toward Sam.

Sam laughed. He spoke and signed, "Levi said he's

one of the frozen chosen."

My eyebrows shot up. I gently shook my head.

"He's an Alaskan Jew. Frozen. Chosen. Get it?" Sam smirked.

I burst out laughing. I liked Levi already.

Levi opened his mouth in a silent laugh and signed slowly, "I want you to meet my sister. She's around here somewhere."

As Levi continued to sign, Sam interpreted for me what Levi said. "I volunteered last year, and I took orientation again in the spring when my sister took it. That's why we weren't on the tour with you."

I nodded and signed, "OK."

A girl with wavy light brown hair appeared at Levi's side as though she'd been watching us.

Levi finger-spelled "Devorah" and then signed "D" and "sister."

"Dev," she said.

"Hi. I'm Wendy." I stuck out my hand and smiled.

She shook it once without smiling. "Nice to meet you."

Someone in charge started calling out names. Levi poked Sam in the ribs and signed something to him about girls. Sam and Levi turned away and left Dev and me to size each other up.

"Where are you from?" Dev's face still held no expression.

She'd probably never have wrinkles. I'd be loaded

with them.

"Louisiana." Surely that would start a conversation.

She glanced at my crucifix and squinted. Then she nodded once and walked away to join Sam and Levi.

Did that mean we wouldn't be friends?

By that afternoon, all the volunteers had gotten a glimpse into the dozens of jobs and hundreds of chores it took to keep the center running. I worked my way to the front of the crowd each time someone demonstrated something I was interested in, like anything having to do with direct contact with the animals. Sam and Levi seemed to prefer the tasks that took muscle. I was convinced they just wanted the most chances to show off in front of the girls. Devorah hung toward the back for every demonstration, like nothing appealed to her.

On the ride home with Sam, I tried to compare Devorah to the handful of other girls I'd met during the day. All from Alaska, the others had been friendlier. But to say "friendlier" implied that Devorah was somewhat friendly, which she wasn't. The only thing I noticed they had in common was a self-reliant attitude, only in Devorah, it was more an I-don't-need-you attitude than an I-can-depend-on-myself attitude.

A question formed in my mind: Did Sam think

down to three and let me have the final say in choosing. Mr. Tony made popcorn for us. Sarah brought me a throw to keep me warm.

I motioned for Sarah to sit next to me, and I covered us both with the throw. Just like when Mom and ' used to watch TV together under one of her flea-market qui s.

Miss Theresa placed a box of tissues next to me, 'nd I thanked her. The movie was a romantic comedy. W 'y was it called a comedy if it makes a girl cry?

Everything the Villaturos did seemed well thought out. They were a family that planned every detail, even to watch a movie. They probably rarely made mistakes or changed their minds. Learning that about them made me feel special that they'd invited me to stay in their home.

3 Things to Forget

Chapter 4

The next morning, I prayed the whole time while Sam drove us to the center. I did not want to work with Devorah. Of all times and places, this was when and where I needed to be near a friend—or at least someone friendly.

A whole country, Canada, separated me from the lower forty-eight states and my friends and family. Alaska, though beautiful, came off as wild and strange. Sam's family was nice, but I wouldn't get to visit Mrs. V every day like I did when we were neighbors. And the guarantee of being with Sam at least part of the time each day didn't prevent the homesickness I was beginning to feel.

I was homesick for my dogs. My stepsister, Alice. Mom. And... well, David, a little.

Never would I admit my homesickness to Sam or his family. They were courteous enough not to ask. And I hated admitting missing David even to myself.

At the center, I received my first assignment on the work schedule, which took my mind off home. Maintaining temporary animal housing for newly rescued small animals and birds.

With Devorah.

Not quite as bad as shoveling dung, but almost. However, I wasn't about to let her get the best of me.

"Why are you so cheerful all the time?" Devorah frowned as we hosed out empty birdcages and small animal kennels. At least she had some kind of expression on her face for a change.

"I'm just glad to be here, I guess. Fortunate and grateful to be here, actually." I'd come so close to not being there at all, but Dev didn't need to hear my long and embarrassing money-problem story.

Still frowning, she shook her head as though the concept of gratitude was foreign to her. Or maybe gratitude for being in this particular place was. So far, Dev and her brother seemed like polar opposites. Levi hadn't complained about being assigned the worst jobs on the schedule, in my opinion, and he always wore a smile.

"Is there something you don't like about being here?" I kept my facial features relaxed to hide the fact that I felt sorry for Dev. She seemed only able to see the negative aspects of everything.

She stopped her hose sprayer, straightened her back, and faced me. "It's not that I don't want to be here, exactly. I just don't like my whole life being controlled. It

kind of conversation, but there was no turning back now. I took another sip of my drink and met her eyes with mine.

Her voice lowered. "I wanted to have sex, but I couldn't do it because I knew how horrified and disappointed my parents would be if they found out. I told my boyfriend so, and he broke up with me because I wouldn't."

It took every ounce of self-control to keep from grimacing. "That must have been devastating."

Her eyes filled with tears. "It was. I thought he loved me."

At least my relationship with David hadn't gotten that far. He'd said he loved me. Would he be the type who'd be willing to wait or not? Maybe it was a good thing for David and me to be apart for a while. Because I would definitely want to wait. But who knew what a couple might be tempted to do if they stayed together long enough? More and more, it seemed important that both the boy and the girl have a belief in God and a strong relationship with Him. Sounded like Dev and that boy she knew didn't have either.

I asked gently, "Can you talk with your mother about this?"

Her eyes grew huge, and she shook her head violently. "No. See what my religion does to me? The guilt? Maybe I should've just done it with him."

"No, no." I rattled my head and stifled the *No!* I wanted to shout. "My religion guides me too. And I wouldn't want to disappoint my parents either. Feeling guilty is normal, I think. Have you been able to talk to anyone else? Maybe your rabbi or a teacher or school counselor?"

Picking at the tabletop's cracked surface, she shook her head slowly. "Anyone who is Jewish would be shocked and maybe even tell my parents. And no one I know who isn't Jewish would understand why I feel so bad, even though he and I didn't ..."

"I understand." I didn't know if either of her generalizations about Jews and non-Jews were fact. I hadn't done anything close to what Dev might have, but I put myself in her place, riddled with guilt and afraid to talk to my mother or priest about it.

I touched her hand. "I'm sorry. This has to be rough. You can talk to me anytime, if you think it would help."

"Thank you." She blinked once, slowly, and withdrew her hand. She folded her arms across the table and rested her head on them.

We sat in silence for several minutes. Poor Dev. Didn't she have any girlfriends to confide in? I was no more than a stranger, but I was glad I let her open up to me. She must've needed someone to talk to pretty badly. If only I could help her feel better. But this subject was out my realm of knowledge and experience on a number of levels. I'd have to do research or talk to an adult about it myself.

A volunteer coordinator approached us with a

wrinkled brow and mouthed to me, "Is everything okay?"

I nodded. I'd been aware of being supervised by the adults all along and blamed it on my being the youngest volunteer there.

Other girls passed by our table and glanced at us. All about Dev's age. What were their dating stories? Did they have regrets?

I'd once feared my friend Jennifer might go the route Dev had, maybe further. That boy who'd caused her to be injured in a car wreck and put in the hospital was history, but what about the next boy she went out with? And my stepsister, Alice... she loved my cousin Jerome so much. But she wouldn't do anything stupid, would she? Would he? It was time to call Alice and Jen to check in and see how things were going for them.

Dev raised her head, revealing red marks from the pressure of her arms. Then she got to her feet and motioned for me to go back to work with her.

3 Things to Forget

Chapter 5

Dev's problems stayed on my mind, which caused Jen and Alice to burrow in too. At the end of the day as Sam and I headed home, I phoned both of them but didn't reach either one. Instead of leaving voice mail, I texted them individually.

To Jen: HOW ARE YOU FEELING? HOW'S PHYSICAL THERAPY? MISS YOU.

To Alice: HOW IS BAYLOR MUSIC CAMP? DO YOU LIKE TEXAS? MISS YOU.

Alice replied right away: I MISS YOU TOO. CAMP IS OK.

Me: THAT'S IT? ONLY OK?

Alice: THE CITY OF WACO IS NICE. THE BAYLOR CAMPUS IS BEAUTIFUL. BUT MY ROOMMATE IS DIFFICULT.

Me: SORRY. CARE TO ELABORATE?

Alice: SHE'S MEAN TO ME. ANGRY ALL THE TIME. I DON'T UNDERSTAND WHY. I'D RATHER TALK SO WE CAN HEAR EACH OTHER'S VOICES. CAN I CALL YOU AFTER

DINNER?

Me: YOURS OR MINE?

Alice: RIGHT. BIG TIME DIFFERENCE. I'LL TRY YOU BEFORE I GO TO BED.

Me: GREAT. WE SHOULD BE FINISHED WITH DINNER BY THEN.

Alice: GOOD. I REALLY NEED TO HEAR YOUR VOICE.

Me: SAME HERE. DON'T LET HER GET YOU DOWN. STAND UP FOR YOURSELF. TELL HER OFF!

Alice: I'VE WANTED TO, BUT YOU KNOW THAT SAYING? BE KIND TO UNKIND PEOPLE. THEY NEED IT MOST.

Me: I DON'T KNOW IF I COULD EVER BE AS GOOD AS YOU! LOVE YOU. TALK TO YOU LATER.

Alice: LOVE YOU TOO. BYE.

Jennifer returned my text with a brief one.

I'M RESTING AFTER PHYSICAL THERAPY. IT'S HARD. MISS YOU TOO. CAN'T WAIT TO SEE YOU AGAIN.

My phone rang its Cajun tune in my jeans pocket as I helped clear the dinner table and scrape the dishes.

I wiped my hands and checked the caller ID. "It's my sister, Alice."

Miss Theresa smiled. "We'll finish the rest. I know it's not easy for you and your sister to get a chance to talk when it's convenient for both of you."

"Thanks." I answered the call and trotted to my room.

"Hey." Alice's voice sounded drowsy, and I pictured her propped against bed pillows in a tiny dorm room.

"What's going on at music camp?" I couldn't

imagine anyone more deserving of the opportunity to be there. She'd dreamed of it for so long, it needed to be great.

"It's educational, in a lot of ways."

"Like …"

"My roommate has a chip on her shoulder."

"Why? Like how?"

"She's blind and a little sensitive about it, among other things."

"Blind? Really. At a music camp." What were the odds Alice would be living with a blind girl while I was living at the home of a deaf boy?

"There are a lot of famous blind musicians, you know."

"True. Some of them must've gone to music camps. She's not there right now, is she? Pretending to be asleep?"

"No, silly. She's taking a shower." Alice sighed. "Anyway, she doesn't seem to trust people much."

"Oh?"

"She acts tough, defensive, like I'm out to get her or something. I can't seem to say anything right."

"So, what's her story?"

"She's being raised by her grandfather because her mother died. Her father took off right after she was born. And honestly, some people here are mean to her."

"But not you, I'm sure. You'll win her over."

"I'm trying. There's always more to a person's story

than you think when you first meet them."

"Mm-hmm." Maybe there was more to Dev's story too.

But, the main reason I wanted to talk—Alice and Jerome. "Have you talked to Jerome lately?"

She giggled. "Ye-e-es. Guess what he said. No, don't guess. You'd never get it."

"Okay. I won't try."

"He said he imagined us always being together." She squealed.

"Wow, he's got it bad." Obvious to me all along.

"Always. Being. Together. Isn't that intense?"

"It is intense."

"I'm fifteen now, so after I get back home, we can go out once every weekend."

"Right. I'm so envious."

"He wanted to come to Baylor and get me to sneak out with him."

Jerome. I gritted my teeth. "Please don't do that, Alice."

"I won't. It's against the rules to leave the campus except with a chaperoned group."

My insides relaxed. "That's one of the reasons I love you, Alice. You're a rule-follower like me."

She laughed.

We chatted a few minutes longer and then said goodnight.

Maybe I didn't need to worry about Alice and

Jerome. At least not right away.

Dev's attitude toward me softened after our private chat, but pain still showed in the tired look of her eyes, like she carried a huge weight of sadness and guilt on her back. In the past, I'd faced a mirror and seen that same look on my face for different reasons. But at least when I smiled at Dev now, she smiled back.

She and I sat down together at lunch. As she removed her food from a paper bag, an aroma similar to anchovies filled my nostrils. I never got to have anchovies on pizza anymore because no one at my house liked them.

Rudely, I leaned and peered at her selections. "What's that?"

"Bagels and lox. It's kosher."

"Mmm. Smells good."

She laughed. "No gentile ever told me that before. Want some?"

"I'd love to try it." I handed her a plastic knife.

She set a piece on a napkin and passed it to me.

"Thanks, that's yummy. I'll ask my mom if we can have that on Fridays during Lent."

Her eyes sparkled and she smiled a tight smile like I'd said something funny. "We have it at least once a week year-round." She took a bite of a pickle.

"Lucky you."

Dev and I spent the afternoon dusting and tidying up in the gift shop. Late in the day, when the exit of a customer left the shop empty, our coordinator pushed through the front door and grinned at us.

"We just got something I think you ladies will like." With a crook of his index finger, he motioned for us to follow.

He opened the door to a room I hadn't been in before. Two adults sat on the floor, their arms filled with wriggling puppies.

I let out a squeal. "Dev. Puppies!"

She grabbed my arm and her eyes widened. She stared at the pups. "Look at the different colors."

"Aren't they gorgeous?" Their coats ranged in color from near-white to various greys and black.

"Orphaned wolf pups," our coordinator said. "Let's get some formula ready for them. I'll show you how to mix it."

Dev and I followed him into a small kitchen. We paid careful attention as he added ingredients to a base of goat's milk and filled a set of baby bottles.

"For canines, never use cow's milk like humans drink. If you can't get goat's milk, use evaporated milk from a can. But you'll have to add a little sterilized water to that."

Dev and I nodded in unison.

"Make sure the milk drips slowly out of the bottle and doesn't run." He demonstrated by dripping milk onto his wrist from a filled bottle. "We can't let the pups get milk into their lungs because they'll develop pneumonia. The formula needs to feel slightly warm like it would be coming from their mother's body, but not hot."

He dripped the milk onto Dev's wrist and then mine to let us experience the correct temperature.

Back in the room with an adult worker to guide and supervise us, Dev and I each nestled a wolf pup in our arms and teased its lips with a bottle of formula. I couldn't help but remember how my puppy Belle had felt in my arms when she was the age of this wolf pup. Only Belle had been much smaller. And these pups were a bit smellier.

The pups began to suckle their bottles. They pushed their pink front paw pads against our bodies like they would've against their mother's. That was how my puppy, Belle, and her littermates had fed from their mother, Chanceaux.

Dev looked at her female pup and crooned tenderly as she nuzzled its head with her chin. "No mother to love you," she whispered. Then she jerked her gaze up at me as if she suddenly remembered she wasn't alone in the room.

I quickly looked away, hoping she wasn't embarrassed. If Dev had feelings she thought she needed to guard, I could respect that.

My pup finished his bottle, and I placed him on my shoulder to pat his back and burp him. "We'll be their foster moms for a while."

"That doesn't mean they'll feel loved." Dev's voice cracked.

Her sadness almost choked me. Did Dev feel unloved by her mother? I'd believed my dad didn't love me when he and Mom divorced. "Dev, …"

She blinked a few times and set her pup's bottle aside. She took a deep breath and turned to me. "In case you haven't guessed, I'm adopted."

My eyes widened. I hadn't a clue. "No. I didn't know. You and Levi look like biological brother and sister."

"Well, it helps that my birth father was Jewish, but my Bubbe—that's my grandmother—let it slip that my mother wasn't. Because of interpretation of a passage in the Torah, in the book of Ezra, some Jews don't consider me a real Jew."

I squinted in confusion. I'd have to find my Bible and look that up.

Dev sighed. "Anyway, now you know why my parents think Levi is better than me, and they love him more. Because I'm not their real daughter. And I'm not a real Jew in their eyes either."

"Dev, do you really believe they feel that way?"

She nodded and raised her pup to her shoulder.

"I have a stepfather, but I believe he loves and cares about me. Not only is Papa D not my real father, but he's Lutheran and I'm Catholic." If Dev knew anything about the history of the Church, she'd know what that could mean if family members didn't truly love one another.

"I believe they wanted a daughter so badly they accepted one that was half Jewish, and not the half that counted most." She patted her puppy on the back.

"Why don't you ask them about this? I bet they love you a lot more than you think."

She shrugged. "Maybe. At least I know Levi loves me."

I smiled. "Of course, he does. I could tell right away when I met him."

"Besides, someday I'll find my birth parents." Her puppy let out a loud burp. "That'll fix everything."

The confidence in her voice scared me for her. What if she found her birth parents but they never wanted her, didn't want to be found, and didn't love her like she hoped?

We placed our first pups in their crate to sleep and picked up two more. We laughed at their fuzzy faces. How would they ever look scary enough to be wolves?

I kept an eye on Dev the rest of the day, as we fed the whole litter, cleaned up after them, and played with them. Just in case she needed me.

Dev's revelation of her adoption and feeling unloved because of it stayed on my mind on the ride home. I'd never known anyone who was adopted, at least not anyone who'd acknowledged it to me. But I'd watched enough TV shows about adoptions to know that not all stories had happy endings. Sometimes a child was not pleased with who the birth parent turned out to be—and sometimes the biological parent didn't want to see the child. Dev knew her birth father was Jewish and her mother wasn't, but did she have any idea of the identity of either of them? Where they lived? Or if they were caring people who'd care about her?

"You're quiet today." Sam kept his eyes on the road.

I'd been staring out the window when I usually would've been warning Sam of potential dangers on the highway until we got safely back to his house.

"Is that a deaf joke?" I leaned close to him and signed as I spoke.

He laughed but shook his head. "No. I want to know if you feel okay."

Just like when we became friends in Louisiana, each day Sam seemed to know me better than he had the day before. He sensed my moods. Sometimes better than David had.

"I'm fine." But it wasn't easy keeping other people's secrets.

As soon as Sam and I entered the house, I went to my room and phoned Mom. Dev's story made me feel so

56

lucky to have my mother. I never doubted Mom loved me. Hearing her voice helped cheer me up. Only I wished I could see and talk to her in person to ask her advice about helping Dev. Without mentioning any names.

3 Things to Forget

Chapter 6

Sam, Levi, Dev, and I started hanging out together for a while at the end of the day, before Sam and I left for home. The Villaturos ate dinner later in the evening than my family did, and we didn't have to worry about being late for it. Plus, we didn't need to think about darkness falling before we got there, like Alice and I did when we rode our bikes or went running in Louisiana. In June, the sun didn't set in Anchorage until well past our bedtime.

I enjoyed the four of us becoming friends because when Sam and Levi got together, they made me laugh even more than Sam did alone. And I got a lot of ASL practice in, goofing around with the guys.

But Dev. Sometimes she seemed less interested in our little quartet and more interested in a duet with Sam. She took opportunities to engage him in conversation that didn't include Levi or me. I wasn't jealous in a girlfriend sort of way—only in a possessive friend sort of way. My time with Sam was limited, and I wanted to make the most of it. We hadn't been working together during the day, so other than at lunchtime, we might not get to talk to each other between the time we arrived at the center in the morning and the time we left to go home that evening.

But even when it seemed like the four of us were having a good time together, Dev would somehow get Sam apart from the rest of us. She'd start signing at lightning speed with Sam, almost like she knew I wouldn't be able to keep up with everything she said. Like she wanted to tell him things she didn't want me to know. Why was she doing that?

It was, at the very least, inconsiderate for her not to speak at the same time she signed so that I might understand. I couldn't tell what Levi thought about the situation as he watched Dev with Sam, but his eyes narrowed behind his glasses.

I began to imagine the worst possible motives for Dev's behavior. Was she a person who used people, taking their sympathy or support or whatever they were willing to give without giving anything in return? Or was she one of those mean girls who hurt people's feelings if it suited her purpose or made her feel powerful? I didn't want to think bad things about Dev. She might be a little difficult at times because of her emotional baggage, but she needed kindness. Just like Alice's roommate.

Friday afternoon, Dev broke into a spoken conversation between Sam and me. She interrupted me and signed something to Sam. When he kept talking to me, she elbowed me aside.

I was shocked that anyone could be so rude, especially someone I'd been so nice to, but I didn't react. The faster Dev signed, the faster Sam did. He shook his head a lot, redness coloring his cheeks.

Levi joined us and stood near me with his eyebrows drawn together. Dev turned her back toward him and signed close to her body, stopping when he got next to her.

Scowling, Levi slapped her arm from behind and signed, "What?"

I was glad he did that, because she turned around and faced him. Then I could see and read her signs.

"Nothing," she signed. "Something between Sam and me."

Her eyes cut in my direction. Sam avoided my gaze.

It wasn't nothing. No one hides nothing. It was definitely something.

I didn't like being on the outside of a secret, especially when it involved Sam, my only proven friend in Alaska. Not counting Mrs. V, of course, who sometimes wasn't aware anymore that she and I were friends when I visited her. And my month in Alaska was speeding by like the red fox running in the nearby pen.

By my second week at the center, the wolf pups gained weight and grew stronger in spite of Dev showing up late half the time to help me care for them. Volunteers and hired workers weren't lacking, so that wasn't the problem. I just thought Dev would be more considerate, of me and of the orphaned pups, after what she confided in me about her adoption. She must've recognized the similarity between the situations. So, what was keeping her?

The memory of Dev's affection for the female pup she'd fed the day it came in spurred me to find her and talk to her about the pup. To try to resurrect the sweetness in her personality she showed that day. I checked indoors and ran over much of the grounds, dodging obstacles and even tripping in a hole, looking for her. I spotted her walking outside.

Breathing hard, I shouted her name and took long strides toward her. "Dev, we're naming the wolf pups today. Don't you want to name yours?" My heart beat rapidly from the exertion. Wow, I was going to be out of shape for track if I didn't get back to running soon.

"Mine? I didn't claim her as mine. Besides, that's kid's stuff." She walked away, in search of Sam, no doubt.

I headed back toward the pups. In two minutes, she joined me. "I changed my mind."

Maybe Sam helped change it. Or maybe I did.

Trying to figure Dev out exhausted me, but I was

glad to have her.

Dev lifted her female puppy. "I'm naming my puppy *Puah*."

I raised my eyebrows. "How'd you come up with that name?"

"Puah was a Hebrew midwife who defied Pharoah by not murdering newborn Hebrew males."

Wow, she remembered that kind of heavy stuff? I tended to remember mostly pleasant Bible stories.

Dev brought their noses together and spoke the new name softly to her as though it were the most beautiful name in the world.

It sounded a little like the result of a bodily function to me, but at least Dev was interacting with the puppies.

As if she read my mind, Dev said, "It comes from a word meaning 'to be beautiful.'" And when she whispered the name, it sounded affectionate and sweet.

"I'd like a different kind of name for my male pup too."

"If you'd read your Bible, you'd find one easily."

I whined. "I don't have my Bible with me. Can't you recommend one?"

"Okay then." She looked toward her left and then upward, as if a cloud overhead held all the names she knew. "Achiram."

I rolled the strange word around on my tongue, pronouncing it as much like Dev had as I could. "What does it mean?"

"My brother is noble."

"I like it." I smiled. What a fitting name for Puah's brother. It had something to do with the way Dev felt about Levi too, I'd bet.

My ride home with Sam that evening was lonely without much conversation.

"I need to concentrate on the road. I can't look at you. Signing or talking with you is too much of a distraction."

With rarely another car in sight, I didn't buy that. I slumped in my seat and watched him sideways through eye slits. I could almost see the gears turning in his head. What was he thinking about? Or who?

As soon as we got home, he locked himself in his room.

Chapter 7

I lay in bed the next Saturday morning, staring at the ceiling. Homesickness blanketed me like a bayou fog. Without a female friend, I especially missed Alice and our sister-talks. If only I could climb onto her bed like I used to and dump out my worries for her to sort out. If anyone besides Mom could advise me about Dev, Alice could.

But Alice was at home in Louisiana, and Dev was here in Alaska. Should I combine those two worlds? Dev was on the verge of ruining Alaska for me, whether she meant to or not. But by next month, her problems wouldn't affect me. If I told Alice about Dev, then when I got home Alice would want to catch up on everything just when I'd want to forget about Dev. Why let her ruin Louisiana too?

But higher on my mind was my birthday... tomorrow. If only I'd planned my trip better so I could've celebrated it in Louisiana, surrounded by people who'd known me for years instead of months or weeks or days.

And who loved me.

Did the Villaturos even know about my birthday?

I could probably ask Sarah. She'd tell me, but asking her would be... the word Miss Theresa used... *tacky*. Sweet Sarah would tell me if she knew of any plans they had, but if she didn't, she'd ask Miss Theresa out of the goodness of her heart. Then Miss Theresa might feel bad about not planning something. I didn't want the Villaturos to feel obligated to celebrate my birthday because they thought I expected it.

And Sam? I couldn't ask him anything anymore.

My phone vibrated and buzzed from the nightstand.

Alice. Was she home from music camp already?

"Hi, Alice." I perked up and sat straight as a board in my bed.

"Hey. Are you awake?"

"Almost there." I stretched my free arm and both my legs, pointing my toes.

"How's Alaska?"

"Beautiful, just like I expected. How were Baylor U and music camp?"

"Good. I wish you'd been there for the student symphony."

"Me too. I bet you were great."

"Thanks. Pretty good, if I must say so myself. Well, Dad and Mama C said so too." She laughed.

"I hope things with your roommate worked out."

"Yeah, just fine. I'll tell you about it when we're

together again."

"Sounds good."

"Did you hear about Jennifer?"

My heart rattled in my chest. Jen's return text the other day had been short. She was scheduled to take physical therapy all summer. When she got hurt in the wreck, the fault of her then-boyfriend, our whole family prayed she wouldn't have to give up her dream of becoming a professional ballet dancer. It was the most important thing in the world to her.

I swallowed hard. "I haven't heard much. Is she okay?" I gripped the phone tighter and held my breath.

"Yeah, she's doing great."

I exhaled.

"Her physical therapist said she'd be able to start dancing again by the time school starts. I visited her like I promised, and I'm going to therapy with her next time."

I smiled. "Thank you, Alice."

"She's determined, so even if the physical therapist hadn't said so ..."

I laughed. "Yeah, I know, that's Jennifer." I was so glad Jen was in our circle. If I'd written her off when she made new friends last summer in New York, I wouldn't have her in my life again. She and I discovered that no matter how many miles came between us, we'd always want to be friends.

"We both miss you so much. We're already talking about how to celebrate your birthday after-the-fact. Sorry we can't be with you for it."

"Me too. See if Gayle is available to get together with us too, okay?" Gayle had become our friend at the start of high school, and the three of us ran track together. I'd discovered soon afterward that she and I were related.

"Sure. She called and asked me to run with her next week."

"I really miss running with y'all. I can't wait to see everybody again."

"No wild animals chase you in Alaska for exercise?"

A laugh exploded from my throat. "No, but I got to bottle-feed some wolf puppies."

"Ohhh, I wish I could do that."

"I bet. Jen would like it too."

"Well, I've gotta go have lunch with Adam and clean my room. Then make him clean his. That's the worst part of the day."

"I need to get dressed and see what's for breakfast. I'll talk to you later. Love you."

"Love you too. Bye."

I texted Mom an *I-love-you*. She texted back that she was under the dryer at a salon. I should watch for a birthday card in the mail. She missed and loved me and hoped I'd have a happy birthday.

The house was unusually quiet when I left my room to visit the bathroom. No Sam noise. No squeaky Sarah-voice in the hall. Or anywhere.

I dressed and made my way to the kitchen. No Miss

Theresa.

The only sound came from outside. A motor running. I glanced through the window.

Mr. Tony was mowing the lawn, the brim of a straw hat shading his face.

Humph. I was on my own for breakfast. I selected an oat cereal and pulled milk from the refrigerator.

I listened to my own crunching and stared at the microwave clock. They must've had errands to run and wanted to let me sleep. That was nice.

The Villaturos' hospitality was so special. They'd been so kind to me, I needed to return their kindness and help out if I could. I rinsed my bowl in the sink and went back to the bathroom I shared with Sam and Sarah. I picked up the dirty towels and headed to the laundry room.

I tossed the bathroom towels into the washing machine and added a few dirty dishtowels from the kitchen. Then I cleaned the bathroom. No easy task due to Sam's dirt. I convinced myself that some of the black streaks on the counters and smudges in the sinks were from the charcoal he used for his drawings.

Sometime during my chores, the lawnmower quieted. Mr. Tony had disappeared.

The towels were being dried by the time Miss Theresa pulled into the driveway. Sam's and Sarah's heads became visible through the car windows.

Sarah burst in through the back door first, loaded

with shopping bags.

"Hey, Sa—" I didn't even get to make eye contact as she zoomed through the kitchen.

Sam sauntered in and grinned. "Miss me?"

"You wish." But I did miss him. Every day he didn't talk to me. And he had to know that when time stretched ahead for months until I might see him again, I would miss him worse. Did I ever actually tell him so? Did I need to?

Miss Theresa took her time and didn't storm in like her children. Carrying bags of groceries, she still used graceful movements. Maybe she'd been a ballet dancer like Jen.

"Hi, Wendy. I thought you'd like to catch up on your rest, but we didn't mean to be gone so long." She closed the back door with her foot.

I smiled. "No problem. It was nice to sleep a little late."

"Did you find something for breakfast?" She placed her bags on the kitchen counter.

"Yes, ma'am. Need some help?"

"No, I'm fine. Thanks."

I took off to find Sam and see if he'd tell me what he had planned for the day. He and Sarah had closed the doors to their rooms. Well, now what should I do?

In my room, I surveyed the landscape. What a mess. As I straightened things up, one of my ragged fingernails snagged my cardigan sweater. Where was my manicure kit?

I was sitting on the bed shaping my nails with an emery board when my door boomed, sending my heart into a spasm. Emery board in hand, I got up and swung the door wide open.

My face heated, and I scowled at him, tired of him shutting me out unless he felt like talking to me. "What's the matter with you? Don't you know how to knock like a civilized person?"

With a stony look, Sam said. "My mom wants to see you."

My expression neutralized. "Is something wrong?" *Rats!* I forgot to take the towels out of the dryer. Did she have her own laundry to do and I got in her way? Maybe she didn't like me using the machines at all.

Sam didn't answer but turned away. I tossed the emery board on the bed and followed him. He led me to the dining room and flipped the light switch.

"Surprise!" A group shouted.

I screamed and stepped back, clutching my shirt.

All the Villaturos—including Mrs. V—had gathered around the dining room table.

"Happy birthday, Wendy."

"Happy birthday." Mrs. V clapped her hands like a child and giggled.

A decorated chocolate cake and a pile of colorful cards and packages filled the center of the table. And I smelled fried chicken.

"How beautiful."

"Hope you don't mind celebrating a day early." Miss Theresa grinned.

"Not at all. Thank you."

"I asked your mother what your favorite foods were."

"You nailed 'em. Thank you, everybody." I ran around and distributed hugs, starting with Mrs. V.

"Enough," Sam said when I hugged him. "Let's eat."

"You had me worried I'd done something wrong." I fake-punched him.

After chowing down on fried chicken and mashed potatoes with gravy, we cleared away the lunch foods and washed our hands.

"What do you want to open first?" Sarah was practically bouncing off the walls.

"I'll start with that big card on top of the stack. Would you hand it to me please?"

Mailed from Louisiana. I opened the turquoise-colored envelope, and the card was gorgeous. Signed by Mom, Papa D, Alice, and Adam. With a gift card for my favorite department store taped inside. Perfect. I held the card to my chest and then reached for the next envelope.

"Another one from Louisiana?" I muttered. Everyone around the table went dead silent, and all eyes were on me.

The card was decorated with glitter and fanciful illustrations of pink flowers. I opened it, and my heart lurched. David.

3 Things to Forget

My face warmed, but there was no way to hide a blush from the Villaturos.

I hope you're having a good time, David had written inside. *I miss you.*

A squeal almost escaped my throat. If I'd been alone or with Alice or Jen, I would've screamed and jumped up and down. They would've joined in.

What did David mean by sending this card? And how did he do it?

Mom must've given him Sam's address. That meant he cared enough to ask for it, because Mom wouldn't have volunteered the information.

Sarah saved me from myself and said, "Open the other cards, Wendy."

When I finished opening cards, Miss Theresa took a small, beautifully wrapped box from the center of the table and handed it to me. Sam did the same with a similar one. Mr. Tony pushed a larger gift toward me.

The tag on the large gift said it was from Mrs. V. I opened it first and pulled out a pale pink cable-knit sweater.

"Thank you, Mrs. V." I was certain someone else had selected the gift for her to give me, but I kissed her cheek. "It's so pretty. I love it."

She smiled.

I tore the wrapping off the gift from Miss Theresa next.

"It's from Tony, Sarah, and me," she said.

72

What about Sam?

I lifted the box lid and gasped. "A charm bracelet for my puppy charm? How sweet of you to think of that. Thank you so much." I hugged Sarah and her parents.

Sam grinned with his arms folded as I held his gift.

Would this be another joke, like the tee-shirt? I cut my eyes at him as I unwrapped the box.

His eyes twinkled. "I don't want you to forget."

I lifted the lid. Inside the box lay a silver charm in the shape of a map of Alaska.

Through mist in my eyes, I smiled at him. Sam and I were still friends.

He could wait and talk to me again when he felt he was ready.

After we enjoyed the cake, Mr. Tony prepared to take Mrs. V back home.

"Mr. Tony, can you wait just a sec? I want to give Mrs. V something. I'll be right back." I ran to my room, desperate to find something I could give her as a remembrance of me. She'd enjoyed giving a gift so much, maybe she'd enjoy receiving one.

I dumped my purse and tote bag and rummaged through the contents of the dresser drawers.

There. Among the photos I'd brought from home was one of me with the dogs, Belle and Chanceaux. Framed too.

I rushed back to Mrs. V. "This is for you. I've been taking good care of your dog, Chanceaux. The other one in the photo is her daughter, my dog Belle, all grown up."

Wide-eyed, Mrs. V accepted my gift. "Thank you."

I had no way of knowing if she remembered Chanceaux at all.

Mr. Tony patted me on the shoulder and smiled, his eyes soft.

I kissed Mrs. V's cheek and told her goodbye.

Then they were gone.

Saying goodbye to Mrs. V was hard each time. Would it ever get easier? Miss Theresa or Mr. Tony made sure I got to see her several times. One of them had checked on her at the nursing home every few days, and they let me tag along if I was available. I shoved to the back of my mind the goodbye I'd have to say to Mrs. V when I eventually left Alaska and went back home. And that would likely be the final goodbye.

I carried my birthday bounty to my room. On the bed, I looked over the cards again and lingered on the one from David.

The birthday sentiment inside was friendly, but I twisted it this way and that in my mind, trying to make it into something more. He missed me. What did he really mean to say? Did David defy his parents by sending the card to me? Did he miss me so much he was willing to take chances to be with me? Sneak out like Dev did?

Did David still love me like he'd said in April?

Or maybe it was just a birthday card from someone trying to be nice.

3 Things to Forget

Chapter 8

After my birthday weekend, Sam became distant toward me again. Dev and Sam's strange behavior together continued, and I became a spy.

I wasn't pleased with myself. Not at all. But I had to know what was going on. Because the thought that kept entering my mind was making me sick to my stomach.

Were Dev and Sam involved with each other? Or getting close to being involved? She'd almost had sex once before. And she was a girl who felt unloved. That could mean she was desperate for affection.

And Sam was her target.

That had to be it. Otherwise, why would she and Sam disappear so often at the same time?

"Where's Dev?" Levi asked me in sign language when he caught me working alone.

I answered Levi's question with a shrug. That was the best I could do.

My name and Dev's had appeared together on the

work schedule most of the time. I could've turned her in for not showing up when and where she was supposed to, but that wouldn't have helped anyone. Least of all me. If anything, Sam might get mad at me for causing Dev trouble if he'd started a relationship with her.

So I kept my mouth shut but eyes and ears open. I took the longest or most circuitous route wherever I went during the day, inside or out, so I could check every nook and cranny at the center, including much of the accessible grounds.

All the while, I was scared to death I'd catch them doing something. But I kept telling myself that if that happened, Sam should've told me the truth to start with.

Then why did I feel guilty, like I was the one doing something wrong?

Late the next afternoon, after utterly failing to spot the two of them during my round-about trips to perform my tasks, I saw them outside one of the storage buildings. I stepped back, hiding in the shadows.

Dev ran up to Sam, who was pushing a wheelbarrow, and he stopped. The conversation began. Verbal mostly, with occasional ASL if anyone came near. I crept closer but maintained a safe enough distance to keep from getting caught. I heard the words and interpreted the signs for "get together" more than once.

If Dev hadn't come on to Sam—and I believed she had—he would never have gotten together alone with her at all. Not without Levi. She was his best friend's sister. And she was vulnerable. Well, maybe he didn't know her story like I did. But Sam was a good person who wouldn't take advantage of a girl just because she made herself available to him. More like threw herself at him. But no. I couldn't imagine him getting involved with a girl he didn't love.

I thumped my forehead with the butt of my hand. Wait. He was sixteen, wasn't he? Hormones could affect a person's judgment. I'd heard about boys in school, juniors and seniors, who had reputations as players. Sam wasn't like that, though. Was he? No, not that I'd seen. Or did I know him as well as I thought I did? I'd been around him less than two months total, counting the time in Louisiana and in Alaska. I had no idea how he acted around girls at school or anywhere else except the center.

Watching the two of them together, I studied Sam. If I didn't think of him as my friend Sam, but as a guy compared to other guys, I could see how a lot of girls would find him attractive. Broad shoulders, lean muscles, nice face, and hair and eyes any girl would like.

Was I trying to protect him—or myself—by spying on him?

The next day, Sam, Levi, Dev, and I were eating

lunch at the same table. But it was like Levi and I didn't exist to Dev and Sam.

With her back to me, Dev signed to Sam without pausing. The only spoken word—whispered—was his name, like she couldn't help saying it. Finally, he swiveled his body in his seat to turn away from her. Not only did she keep signing to him, sticking her hands in his face, but she started touching him. His shoulder, his arms, his leg.

My face heated.

Levi scowled. "I'm sorry," he signed to me. "She's rude."

I felt like when I walked in on my mom and dad in a private emotional moment before they split up. Very uncomfortable.

Apparently so did Sam. He stood up and stormed off without a word to any of us.

Dev ran after him. What was wrong with that girl? Couldn't she take a hint? If she really cared about him, she'd give him some space to breathe.

Levi and I exchanged glances.

"I miss him and wish I knew what was going on," I signed. I begged him with my eyes to fill me in on what he might know about Sam and Dev.

With a dark look and wrinkles between his eyebrows, Levi stilled the movement of his hands except to finish eating his lunch.

I remained for a minute, toying with my food, but

then got up and threw it into the trash.

Later that afternoon, Sam and I were in the car and almost home when I couldn't hold in my feelings any longer. His facial expression was somber, his eyes tired like he'd been losing sleep. I'd thought that at sixteen, he should seem older. Well, he sure did, now.

I tapped his shoulder to make him turn his head toward me. "Sam, what's wrong?" I signed. "Please tell me."

He faced forward again and stared straight ahead. "I wish I could tell you, but I can't."

I tapped him harder and stuck my face near the steering wheel so he could read my lips. "The way you've been acting... it's like you don't want to be friends anymore."

"How can you say that?" He frowned.

I drew back. He focused on the road.

Arms extended, I signed in front of him as I said, "Did I do something?" I didn't think I had, but maybe I could get him talking.

"It's not about you." He almost shouted.

I spoke and signed. "It's about Dev, isn't it?"

His face reddened. "Let it alone, Wendy. It's none of your business."

That hurt, but I continued my dual communication method. "Then would you please talk to someone else about it?" If it had to do with sex, then... "What about your father?"

Sam's face contorted like I'd never seen it before. "This isn't your concern. Why do you always have to stick your nose into my family's business?"

That drove the knife deep and twisted it. As soon as we pulled into the driveway and stopped, I jumped from the car, slammed the car door and ran into the house. I rushed past Sarah and Miss Theresa without speaking and went straight to my room to hide my tears.

Chapter 9

Sam had said his "family's business." Not "his business." Was he angry because I suggested he talk to his father? Isn't that a natural thing to suggest to a male friend when he's troubled? Otherwise, what did Sam's relationship with Devorah have to do with his family?

A box of tissues in hand, I slumped to the area rug on the floor next to my bed.

Sam was right about one thing. I did stick my nose where it wasn't appreciated sometimes. I didn't start out to; it just worked out that way if I convinced myself that they needed me. I'd done that with Jennifer and with Mr. Tony about Mrs. V.

But just like in those cases, I was worried about someone I cared about. Should I talk with someone else who cared about Sam? But Mr. Tony… he might react badly, like he did when I butted into his handling of Mrs. V after we found out she had Alzheimer's.

A light tapping at my door startled me. It was

probably Miss Theresa or Sarah checking to see if I was all right. I rose to my feet and prepared to offer an apology for my rudeness a few minutes earlier. I took a deep breath, plastered a smile on my face, and opened the door.

"Sam." My smile dropped away.

"May I come in?" The softness in his expression let me know I wasn't in trouble with him.

I stepped aside and swept my arm toward the interior of the room.

He took a few steps in and turned to face me. "I hate that we argued." He hung his head.

I touched his arm, and he looked up. "Me too," I said.

His eyes held no sparkle. He looked worn out. Definitely older.

I left the door open and sat on the floor in the middle of my room.

He joined me and sat, facing me with his arms propped on bent knees.

We stared at each other for a moment.

"I haven't been letting you talk to me much, so you start. Ladies first," he said.

I took a deep breath and let it out. "I've been worried about you, Sam."

"Worried how? Why?"

"You don't seem like yourself." I looked straight into his eyes.

"I have a lot on my mind." He glanced to the side.

84

I snorted. "Sorry, but I can tell that much."

His features remained calm and soft. "Mind if I say something I've noticed about you?"

My eyebrows jerked. "O-kaay …"

"You don't trust easily."

My whole body jerked back, and I placed my hands on the floor to hold myself upright. He was criticizing me when he was the one who'd been acting weird?

"Care to explain?" I used my snarkiest voice, lost on a deaf boy.

"You don't trust your friends to make the right decisions for themselves even if they've proven themselves trustworthy."

I frowned and stood up. "I don't think I like that accusation."

He remained on the floor. "Please, sit back down." He spoke the words with no hint of anger in his voice or his face.

I tightened my lips so that they must've disappeared from view, and I looked to the ceiling. Anywhere but at him.

"Please?" He patted the floor. *Thud, thud.*

I lowered myself again to the floor.

"Don't you trust me?" He reached for my face to make me look at him, and his fingertips brushed my jaw. "I need you to trust me."

I opened my mouth but no words came out.

"I'm not doing anything wrong. And I care what you

think of me."

"But Devorah …"

He dipped his chin and looked up at me. "Trust me."

"I'll try." It was my turn to hang my head.

Alone again, of course I thought of other things I should have said to Sam.

Like, are you praying about whatever it is that's on your mind? Or better yet, let's pray together about whatever you want to.

Duh.

The Villaturos had taken me to Mass with them each Sunday, where we'd agreed to pray for Mrs. V's health. I could only hope Sam had been praying there or alone in his room about his problem.

Or maybe he was fine, and I was the one with the problem.

Trust him, he'd said.

I was determined to trust Sam. After all, I hadn't caught him and Dev making out or even kissing. Never a warm embrace or anything close.

They were just always talking. And talking. And talking. Whether with their voices or with their hands.

He was awfully patient with her. More patient than he'd been with me at times. Had I pushed too hard into his personal concerns? I didn't want to lose Sam as my friend.

With fingers touching the cross around my neck, I knelt at the side of my bed and prayed for Sam, Devorah, and me. And Levi too, because he was caught in the middle of whatever was going on.

I stayed in my room until Sarah called me to come to dinner.

I assumed Sam and Dev's private conversations would taper off after he and I had our talk, but they didn't. After asking me to trust him, Sam seemed more relaxed around Dev. They seemed like they were becoming good friends. Better friends than he and I were?

He spent even less time with me and more time with her. Maybe Sam had chosen Dev's friendship (whatever that might be) over mine. Was he still not doing anything wrong like he'd told me?

Maybe his telling me to trust him was his way of avoiding a confrontation over our disintegrating friendship. He was letting me down easy, so he didn't have to come out and say we weren't such good friends after all. That could be it. Spending time together every day might've changed his mind about me. Did he regret my coming to Alaska?

That question stuck with me, gnawing at my gut. I held back the tears. If it weren't for my responsibility to the puppies, the dam would've burst wide open.

In my room after dinner, I opened my ASL book. If I had to spend time alone each evening, I may as well study. At least I would be better able to interpret Dev and Sam signing to each other.

After an hour, I was thirsty and left my room to get a chilled bottle of water. As I passed down the hall on the way to the kitchen, voices from Sam's parents' bedroom stopped me. Alaskan walls were well insulated, so the voices must've been pretty loud.

Sam, his face flushed, exited the room and softly closed the door behind him. He looked up and saw me. Eyes troubled and without saying a word, he went straight to his own room.

Why did I think they were discussing something about me?

Lord, I'm grateful for the friends I have. I sure would like to keep them.

After seeing Sam come out of his parents' room, my patience with him was fading fast. I sipped on my water as I paced my floor.

My problem was growing beyond not being able to trust Sam with Devorah. I had to know if I was still welcome in his house. Whether Sam wanted me to stay or go home. I might be one of those friends that it was fine having around some of the time but not living under the same roof. And Dev sure didn't act like she cared to have me for a friend at the center. If the only acceptance left for me in Alaska was Mrs. V, who didn't recognize me most of the time, I may as well go home. I could get on a plane tomorrow. I could try, anyway.

I wrote a note and slipped it under Sam's door. *We need to talk.* I stood in the hall and waited, moving back and forth in front of his door. He might notice the movement of my shadow through the crack at the bottom of the door before he noticed the note.

He opened his door after a minute or two. "Come in."

I walked in, my first time in his room. And I stopped. His drawings covered the walls. Beautiful illustrations of animals, buildings, street scenes, mountains. I squinted. Was that one of me?

Who cared? I was too upset to worry about being immortalized in one of Sam's sketches.

I faced him and crossed my arms, the standard closed-off, self-protective body language.

He stared at me.

"Sam, I need to ask you—are you still glad I came to visit?"

His eyebrows practically twisted into a knot. "Of course."

"Then why don't you and I see each other more? You seem to avoid me at work and at home. We've watched one movie together in the evening. One." I held up my index finger, palm facing in, for emphasis.

"I'm not avoiding you. I'm busy at the center, and I'm used to going to my room in the evenings. I like being alone. Sometimes I want to draw. Remember?" He waved a hand toward his work.

Right. That made sense.

I unfolded my arms. "You and Dev seem to disappear at the same time so often during the day."

"Are you keeping watch on me now?" His eyebrows rose as high as humanly possible.

"Well, it's easy to tell when Dev is not where she's supposed to be, which is usually on a task with me."

"So? Then Dev is doing wrong."

"I can't help but notice that you're nowhere to be found sometimes too."

"Do you really want to know where I am when you can't find me?"

"Yes. Yes, I do." The trust thing was out the window.

"I hide out in our volunteer coordinator's office to get away from Dev when she won't let me alone. I'm trying to be nice and not hurt her feelings. But she's bugging me to take her out on a date, and I don't want to do that."

I was speechless.

At first I didn't know whether to be glad for me or to be sad that he couldn't stand up to her.

"Okay." I nodded and left, closing the door behind me. Then I stood in the hall a minute. Had he even told me the truth?

I'd thought my time in Alaska was going to be so

90

spectacular I'd barely think of David, if at all. But I had to be honest with myself. I missed him. Not just the romance. The friendship we'd had too.

The change in Sam and the thing between him and Dev made me think even more of David. I'd imagined all the fun Sam and I would have in Alaska, but it wasn't happening. The memory of good times I'd had with David sneaked into my consciousness like a beetle through a crack in the baseboard. Not a horrible thing, but I still didn't want it there. And seeing Sam as someone another girl might pursue burst the little dream bubble that lurked in the back of my mind. Sam as a potential boyfriend somewhere down the road. Not soon, but someday, if things didn't work out with David. I had a mental list of boys with the character and qualities I liked. Only two had made the list so far.

Was I jealous of Sam? Envious that Dev or another girl might eventually have a relationship with him? That could happen. A guy might finally give in to the pressure.

Or was I jealous because I no longer had a relationship with David?

3 Things to Forget

Chapter 10

The animals became my diversion from all things related to boys. Animal behavior was mostly consistent. Animals never disappointed me. I could always count on them.

Dev surprised me by following the schedule and showing up. With round-the-clock care no longer needed for the wolf pups, she and I worked with some of the small, permanent animal residents that wouldn't be able to return to the wild. The one-winged eagle and three-legged porcupine were our favorites. Dev really took to the disabled animals. I knew she had a soft heart under her hard shell.

Maybe Sam had finally convinced her that he really wasn't interested.

Sam grinned all during breakfast Saturday. Finally, he looked at me and said, "We need to do something fun together."

I turned my head and looked past my shoulder behind me and then at Sam again. "Are you talking to me?" I pointed at myself for emphasis.

He laughed. "Yes, I am."

"Do something… like what?"

"I haven't exactly been a good host, so you can choose what we do. We don't have a lot of days left together."

Right on both counts. "I didn't bring my tiara for the opera."

"No, wait. I take back what I said. I don't have much money, so I'd better choose."

"No. I'd like to dress up a little. It's been a long time. Please?"

"Would you like to eat dinner in a restaurant?"

"I'd love it. Just the two of us?"

"Just the two of us. Tonight."

"Dress up. And shower first." I pinched my nose with a thumb and index finger.

Was this a date?

"You look nice." Sam surveyed me from the top of

my hair down to my black flats and up again.

"Thanks." I clutched the hem of my swingy dress, the only one I'd brought to Alaska. I'd worn it to church once but felt overdressed. Most of the congregation had worn casual clothes.

My hair held smooth, loose curls, and I'd applied a little makeup. Neither of those had been practical for working with wildlife.

"You look so pretty," Sarah whispered to me.

I smiled and said, "You're prettier. I can't wait to see a picture of you after school starts."

"I'll send you one of me wearing my new outfit for the first day of school."

"Are we finished?" Sam grabbed his mom's car keys off the kitchen counter.

I rolled my eyes.

Sarah said, "Be glad you don't have a brother."

"Have a good time." Miss Theresa kissed both Sam and me on the cheek.

Mr. Tony stepped into the room. "Drive carefully, son."

"I will, Dad."

"I'll make sure he does." I grinned behind Sam's back.

Sam opened the door and let me pass through first. A real gentleman. And it was nice that he asked to use his mom's car, a newer (and cleaner) one than his.

The Italian restaurant we had decided on was the

perfect choice. The aromas and atmosphere were both delicious. Just right for a first date.

Was this really a date? Or simply an outing to reward a hardworking friend before she had to leave and go back home?

Sam's carefully combed hair and pressed button-down shirt fit the first category. Sam + Italian restaurant + pressed shirt = romance?

My hands got jittery. I splashed water when I picked up my glass from the table. Maybe I wasn't used to my new charm bracelet on my wrist. I took a quick sip and unrolled my napkin, allowing me to dry my hand without making a big deal of it.

Sam didn't seem to notice my nervousness.

The waitress brought a basket of breadsticks. "Do you need a little more time to order?"

"Yes, thank you." Sam gave her a sunny smile.

If this was a date, did I want it to be? Sam's figure as he studied the menu across the table slowly morphed into David's.

"See anything you like?" Sam peered over the menu at me.

I double-blinked, and warmth rose to my cheeks. "Oh, everything looks good. But it's been a long time since I've had my mom's chicken parmigiana, so I think I'll have that. What about you?"

"Spaghetti and meatballs. I could eat it every day."

"How original." I grinned so he'd know I was

teasing.

"Geniuses like to simplify their daily lives to devote their energy to more creative endeavors."

"I see. How else do you simplify your daily life?"

"I follow a routine."

"It never changes?" I bit the end of a breadstick.

"I change it for emergencies." He lifted his water glass as if in a toast. "And special people."

Being called special filled me with satisfaction like the warm bread in my hand.

Sam parked his mom's car in the garage, the headlights reflecting off the wall of Mr. Tony's hanging hand tools. We both stared straight ahead for an awkward length of time. Was he thinking about kissing me? We'd had one brief kiss in Louisiana, last fall when he said goodbye to me before he flew back home.

I held my breath, not a good idea if I was about to be kissed and would have to hold it for that. I let the air out quietly.

His face partially illuminated, his eyes caught in the reversed light of the headlights like a wild animal, he waited a few seconds. He killed the engine. Rigid like a statue, his hands gripped the steering wheel.

He must've been trying to figure out what to do. Did

he think I expected to be kissed? I couldn't stand the thought of a pity kiss. Especially after the genuine, spontaneous kiss of months ago.

For both our sakes, this awkward situation couldn't continue. I opened my door to let him off the hook. "We'd better go inside."

Sam exhaled, having no idea how loud it sounded.

I scowled in the dresser mirror at my droopy hair and fading makeup. So much for my first and probably only date in Alaska. I slipped off my flats and then my dress, sniffing it for food or body smells. Not bad. It could be worn again without washing. I hung the dress in my closet.

Leaning over the bathtub, I washed my face and hair under the faucet. Like that ancient song Mom said her mother used to sing to her after she had a bad date, "I'm gonna wash that man right out of my hair."

But I couldn't wash Sam out of the inside of my head.

At least for the time being, Sam was my friend. If I didn't mess it up. No guarantee comes with any friendship. And just because he took me out to eat didn't mean he felt anything stronger than friendship.

Besides, I'd be gone soon. When separated again by

4500 miles, we'd have only one thing in common, Mrs. V. Well, three things if I counted our love of animals and art. But if something happened to Mrs. V… I shuddered under my dripping hair. Without that connection to her, would Sam and I remain friends?

Sam hadn't done anything bad to me, hadn't broken any promise or appointment, and yet I'd given my friend a hard time. So what if he spent time with someone else during the day? Devorah or anyone. I wouldn't want to be friends with someone who demanded a certain number of hours from me each day. Who would want that from a girlfriend—or boyfriend either? And after working at the center and driving us home, didn't he deserve to spend part of his free time with his art?

I needed patience. I needed to trust him like he'd asked.

And if he made a mistake, would I stick by him? Try to help him no matter how bad the mistake? Help him get on the right path again?

He'd never given up on me. And I'd made mistakes. Some big ones.

I would just have to work this out with him.

3 Things to Forget

Chapter 11

Devorah's improved behavior didn't last long.

"This might not be a paying job, but it's still a job." I dropped a bucket of feed to the ground.

Dev glanced at me from the rock where she sat with her legs extended and ankles crossed.

"And I expect you to pull your weight." I placed my fists on my hips as I glared at her.

"Can't you see I'm on the phone? I'm taking a break."

"Can't you see the animals need to be fed and watered on a schedule? At a regular job, you might not get a break at the exact moment you want it or even get one."

She mumbled into her phone and then lowered it to her lap. "What do you think happens when we're not here? The center has people paid to do what we do. And look at all the other volunteers." She waved her hand in the direction of some of the other teens, busy doing what they were supposed to be doing.

"Right now this is our job, paid or not. Do you get paid for everything you do at home?" I picked up the bucket. Why did I bother asking? She was probably one of those spoiled, ungrateful princesses, and she didn't have to do anything at home to contribute. My heart thudded, and heat rose up my neck to my face.

"Well, maybe I deserve a rest." She smirked at me.

"A rest? You're a slacker." I'd never called anyone a name straight to her face before. Already, guilt oozed into my thudding heart.

"Maybe I don't care. I just want to do what I want to do." She flipped her hair back.

"Just because you don't like that your parents made you volunteer doesn't mean you can take it out on the rest of us or the animals."

She frowned. "I'm not hurting anybody. If you're so worried, you go feed the animals." She dismissed me with a flip of her hand and picked up her phone.

"Have you ever thought about anyone or anything other than yourself for more than a few minutes?" I turned on my heels and hurried to make it in time for the next feeding.

I'd had about all of Dev's attitude I could take. I hurried through my remaining stops.

Having rehearsed what I planned to say, I marched to my coordinator's office. By a stroke of good luck, I found him there at a desk.

102

"Excuse me." I stood straight and tall to show some serious dedication to my job—and authority to be in his office.

He looked up with a soft expression. "Hi, Wendy. What can I help you with?"

"Has Devorah been reassigned to work with someone else? Because she's rarely with me, in spite of what the schedule says."

"Really."

"I'd just like to know. I, um, miss her." I shifted my feet and laced my fingers together.

He cleared his throat. "I'll look into it." He stood. "Is that all?"

"Yes. Thank you." I marched back out.

At last I'd taken a stand against Dev's poor conduct. For the sake of the animals, of course.

Later that afternoon, Devorah's face was cayenne-pepper red. She stormed up to me on the grounds. "Thanks a lot, you little snitch. And the word that rhymes with it."

My jaw dropped. It had been only an hour or so since I'd talked to the coordinator.

"Don't act like you don't know what I'm talking about." She practically growled in my face. Some of her spit hit me. I wiped my cheek.

Was she the type to physically strike? My eyes searched each side of me for backup.

No one appeared close enough to hear. I kept my mouth shut. Anything I said might incriminate me. And she might actually bite.

My eyes met Levi's a distance away, coming up behind Dev. He hurried over and stepped between Dev and me. I realized I hadn't breathed since she showed up.

She tried to shove Levi out of her way but failed. She stepped around him for another verbal assault. "Do you know what you did? My parents are coming to get me. I'm out of the volunteer program because of you."

I thought that's what she wanted.

Her arms shot through the air toward my neck. I took a step backward.

Levi tackled her, and they both hit the ground. Arms and legs cut the air. Levi tried to pin Dev's arms as she tried to kick him and scratch his face. From the looks of it, their fight was the type of sibling battle this brother and sister had experienced before.

Levi's glasses flew off. I backed up even more and picked up his glasses. Other volunteers became aware of the scuffle and gathered around.

Between grunts and groans during the struggle, Dev yelled, "You're just jealous of Sam and me. Admit it."

I gasped. How could she say that in front of all these people? Embarrassed for both her and me, I scanned the

you. Did you know I suspected for a while that you might have sex with her?"

Sam's head jerked back, his eyes huge. "Seriously? Don't you know me better than that?"

"I thought I did, but you were so secretive."

"I wasn't supposed to tell anyone. Dev has no idea exactly who her birth parents are."

I slapped the edge of my seat. "You have to tell her. She needs to know her biological family is so close. She wants to search for her birth parents because she feels unloved by her adopted parents. She thinks they love her less because she's only half Jewish."

"She does? Levi never mentioned that."

"Maybe he doesn't know she feels that way."

"And Levi loves her. I love her too, because she's my cousin, not in the way she thinks she wants of me. But anyway, I can't tell her anything."

"Somebody has to." I tilted my head and eyed him.

"My parents won't let me." He set his mouth in a firm line.

I twisted my mouth to the side.

He shook his head. "No, Wendy... not you. You can't tell her."

I wasn't making any promises just yet. "Is that why you were in your parent's room the other day when I saw you come out? You were talking with them about how to handle the situation with Dev?"

"Yes."

"Don't you know the trouble that could've been avoided if someone had told her what you just told me?" Not to mention worry on my part.

"I understand, but my mother promised her sister not to tell the child the facts. Then my aunt and the birth father died. And I promised—"

"What?" I slapped a hand on my forehead. "They're both dead?" This was a big old stinkin' whole story after all.

Sam nodded. "Yeah. Car accident."

"This is horrible." My eyes scrunched.

He shook his head gently. "I've been trying to figure out what to do. I didn't want to hurt Dev by rejecting her without a reason, and I don't want to hurt her now."

"I get it. How do you tell a girl that you, her brother's friend, know who her birth parents are? But they're dead. And in the same breath …"

"She's been hitting on her cousin."

"She'd be devastated, humiliated."

"I know. More uncomfortable than I was each time she hit on me." He chuckled.

I appreciated his trying to lighten the mood. But, man. What a difficult situation.

However, Dev's adopted parents may not have promised anything to anybody.

Sam drove us home, his eyes on the road without fail. But he was thinking about Dev, I had no doubt.

I listened to the radio a little while and then turned it

off. Sam glanced at me, and I caught his eye.

"How did Levi's parents wind up adopting a baby from your mother's sister?" I signed the best I could as I spoke.

Sam answered slowly, as though collecting the information from the farthest corners of his memory. "I was a little kid at the time but learned about it later. When my mom found out from my aunt that the baby's father was Jewish, she thought of Levi's parents right away. They were the only Jewish friends our family had, and Levi's mother didn't think she'd be able to have more children. She wanted another child."

"Wasn't your aunt a Christian?"

"No. My aunt was a wild teenager. S' . didn't practice any faith at all. That's what mʸ ɔm told me when I was old enough to understand."

"She and the boy were both young ..."

"Yeah. Mom said there was no way they would've been able to care for that baby."

"But the baby could have been placed for adoption with one of the big agencies, a Catholic or even a non-denominational Christian one." I had to fingerspell the words I was afraid Sam couldn't lip-read.

"My mom wasn't Catholic at the time, even though Dad has always been. I'm not even sure she was a practicing Christian. She just wanted to find a good family she knew, one close by, to adopt the baby. The baby was part of our family, and my mom didn't want to lose track of her. Deep down, she hoped someday when my aunt was older, she'd want a relationship with her little girl."

"But then she died." Tears gathered in my eyes. I found some paper napkins in the glove compartment and wiped my eyes and nose.

Sam's face held pain in the set of his mouth and squint of his eyes.

To allow Sam to watch the road, I signed near the dashboard as I spoke, "How long have you known Levi?" It translated to "How long you know Levi?" I didn't need to ask how long Sam had known Dev. I could figure that out myself.

"We've been in deaf school together since first grade."

"Is he your best friend?"

He smiled. "Well, he's the only friend I told about you after I met you."

Warmth filled me from head to toe.

I grinned and continued to sign near the dashboard. "What did you say about me?"

"You're smart, caring, and talented. You know, the usual stuff I say about girls."

I fake-punched him, and he laughed.

"Do you visit his house?" I signed near the dashboard again.

"I visited there a lot before high school. Lately we've seen each other mostly at school, extracurricular activities, and sports events. And deaf basketball practice."

I stared through the windshield.

"Wendy, what are you thinking?"

"We should visit Levi and Dev, don't you think?"

"Why?" He gripped the steering wheel tighter, his knuckles whitening.

Really, guys could be so clueless sometimes. "Dev must feel awful. She's going through a rough time. She's not a bad person. I don't think she's a bad person, and I want her to know that."

"See? Caring." He turned his thumb toward me.

"What about you?" I propped my hands on the dash after signing.

"Yeah, I'm the caring type too." He stuck his nose in the air for a moment.

"Right."

He didn't exactly commit to a visit, so I had my work cut out for me.

3 Things to Forget

Chapter 12

Sam and I agreed not to mention Dev, or the day's incident and resulting boot-out, to his parents. They were better off not knowing. Otherwise, we might have two sets of parents upset.

After dinner, Sam and I headed toward our separate rooms.

He touched my arm and stopped in front of his door. "I need to draw."

"I know you do. I need to write some things down to help me sort them out."

"Drawing helps me sort things out."

I nodded, and he turned his doorknob.

From my travel bag stored in the closet, I withdrew a notebook. I'd planned to write down all my experiences in Alaska and had filled the first few pages with my initial reactions to the mountains, my first visit with Mrs. V, and the first few days at the center. But that's as far as I got. I hadn't planned on being so physically tired from work or emotionally tired because of Dev by each evening.

Even though I wouldn't have to see Dev anymore, I needed to figure out a plan for talking to her and straightening things out between us. I could write some dialogue for what I'd say, what Dev might say, and what I'd say in response. I'd practice it like I'd practiced what to say to John-Monster and to the Sticks in eighth grade.

Two hours later, I had something worthwhile on paper. But my plan wouldn't work without Sam's cooperation, the biggest part being that he'd have to drive us to Levi and Dev's house. I texted a request for admission to Sam's domain.

Me: CAN I VISIT YOU IN YOUR ROOM?

Sam: WHEN?

Me. NOW?

Sam: GIVE ME A MINUTE.

Me: OK

In exactly one minute, notebook under my arm, I knocked nice and loud at his door. The vibration from the knock might be visible to him. Or he'd feel it like I did when he knocked on my door. Without hesitation, I opened his door.

"Hey!" He hastily covered an easel with a torn, stained bed sheet. "I said give me a minute."

"It's been a minute." I used a calm tone.

His face colored. "I didn't mean that literally."

I shrugged. "I'm literal."

"I don't like anyone to see my artwork before it's

116

finished." He moved the easel, facing it toward a wall.

"That's fine. I don't need to look." Why was he making such a big deal about it?

"Good." He stretched his arms straight above his head and groaned.

I turned his only chair around, the one at his desk, and sat facing him. I held my notebook on my lap.

"Want a cola?"

"Yes. Diet, thanks."

He took off. I stood up and walked around his room to get a closer look at his drawings on the walls. They were incredible, even better than the drawing he did of Mrs. V and me last year. His art was fine art. My art, like the set designs for the eighth-grade musical, was commercial and amateurish.

I studied the sketch of the girl I'd thought might be me, last time I was in his room. But on close inspection, it didn't look much like me at all. Did he know another girl with a long nose, long dark hair, and dark eyes with light flecks in them?

He returned in less than five minutes with two glasses of cola with ice. He handed me one and then sat on the edge of his bed.

I took a sip of my drink and set it on the desk. "I have a plan for talking to Dev that won't be embarrassing for you or for her."

"Wait a minute. You seriously want me to go over there?"

"Well, duh. How else would we show her we care about her after what happened? Write her a letter?"

"I was thinking about it." He had a goofy grin on his face.

"Nope. That won't work. It has to be in person." I held my head erect.

He lowered his chin and looked at me from under his eyebrows. "Who will do the talking?"

"I will. You only have to drive me there. And go in with me."

"Whew." He swiped a hand across his forehead and gulped his drink.

"I figure I don't mention you at all."

"Sounds good so far." He set his empty glass on a nightstand.

"After I smooth things over between us, I'll convince Dev that she needs to talk to her parents about the things she's told me that bother her. Especially about feeling she's not loved as much as Levi because she's adopted. With the trouble she got into at the center, they'd want her to talk to them, I think. My parents would. She needs to tell them the stuff she's been holding deep inside."

I'd known too many who hadn't confided in someone—and the horror that resulted. If I'd known John-Monster was suicidal or Tookie had an eating disorder, I either would've talked with them or told an adult before it was too late. At least I think I would have. I would now in the same situations.

118

"How are you going to get Dev to open up to her parents like that?" Sam crossed his arms.

"I have the dialogue right here that I'm going to use." I tapped the notebook with a fingernail.

"I hope you won't try to get her to talk to her parents about wanting to be with me. They would be shocked, and who knows what they'd say. And the embarrassment for her …"

"No, I won't. But I doubt she'd tell her parents about wanting to date you."

"Why not?"

"She told me they didn't plan to let her date non-Jewish boys."

"So why was she trying to get me to take her out?"

Had I said too much? I'd promised Dev not to tell Sam the things she'd told me. She feared he would tell Levi. But she'd crossed some lines, doing harm to her reputation and her friendships. I owed Sam this explanation because this situation involved him, and telling him would help him understand how important this trip to see Dev really was.

"Based on what she's done in the past, she would've sneaked out with you."

He grimaced and rubbed the back of his neck. "What a mess."

Did he mean Dev or the situation? I pointed an index finger at him. "Don't tell Levi about that. I want to help Dev, not make things harder for her."

"Okay, I won't."

I looked at him hard, with my eyes narrowed.

"I promise." He placed his hand over his heart.

"Good. Here's my plan. Once I get her to agree to talk to her parents about her insecurities at home and her attitude at the center, I'll suggest that she ask them about her birth parents. Then if her parents tell her the truth, she'll know to leave you alone. She won't have to be embarrassed because she won't know that you know her birth mother was your aunt. She died when you were too young to remember, and Dev won't know your mom told you about it later. Sound reasonable?"

Sam nodded. "Can I read the dialogue myself instead of you reading it to me, so I don't have to read your lips? I'm tired."

"After I read it aloud. I want to hear how it sounds to my own ears. And I've always wanted to see how much you understand of what I'm saying by reading my lips. You can let me know when you compare that to reading it yourself. Okay?"

"You're strict, but okay."

"By the way, when did your parents tell you about your aunt being Dev's birth mother?"

"Around the time Levi and I starting hanging out together every day. About twelve years old."

"You're good at keeping secrets long-term."

He grinned. "I know."

I opened the notebook, faced him squarely, and began to read aloud.

At breakfast the next morning, I caught Sam by himself. I signed as I said, "Good morning."

He gave me a single wave, his other hand occupied by a spoon.

I had his attention, so I spoke. "There's one thing I forgot to mention last night."

"Whah?" He said through a mouthful of milky cereal.

"You'll have to be the one to ask Levi if we can come over."

Sam frowned and swallowed. "I have to?"

"I can't do it. Levi is your friend, not mine. At least not a close enough friend for me to invite myself to his house."

He sighed. "Yeah, you're right. Maybe he'll be back at the center today, and I can ask him."

"And if he isn't?" I had to plan for any obstacles to our visit so I could remove them if possible.

"I'll wait one more day and text him."

"Thank you." I could've kissed him. Instead I smiled and poured myself some cereal.

Levi returned to the center that day.

Sam got to him immediately after he arrived and gave him a bear hug. "I'm glad you came back, Levi." Sam signed as he spoke.

I gave them their space, hanging back but watching for a minute. They signed to each other fast, and I couldn't keep up at a distance. I trusted that Sam was working out a plan with Levi for us to visit Dev, so I moved on to find out who my new volunteer partner would be.

At lunch, Sam swung his long legs over his seat and sat next to me. "It's arranged. We're going to their house Sunday after lunch."

"Sunday? Why not Saturday?"

"Saturday's the Jewish Sabbath."

"Of course. I forgot about that."

"Good thing we're allowed to go to their house on our Sabbath."

"Yeah, good thing. Did Levi say how Dev is doing?" I took a bite of my sandwich, pieces falling from it.

"He saw his parents yelling at her. She's been hiding in her room since then, not talking to him or anyone." Sam unwrapped and laid out his food.

"I can relate." I wiped mayo from my chin.

"He thinks she's embarrassed and may not want to face us."

I moaned. "I've known that feeling. How did you get

122

him to agree to let us come over?"

"Their mom and dad will be visiting friends, and he thinks that us talking to Dev without the parents around would be good for her."

"What if she won't see us?"

"He said he knows how to get her out of her room." Sam popped a potato chip into his mouth.

Brothers knew how to do that stuff, I supposed.

I couldn't have hoped for better circumstances for our little meeting. Now it was up to me.

Please guide me, God, and let it go well.

3 Things to Forget

Chapter 13

Sunday morning I woke early so I could practice my dialogue before getting ready for church. I paced the floor as I practiced. Good thing I wasn't a nail biter because this would've been a time anyone would chew one down to the quick.

Afterward, I showered, dressed, and went to the kitchen for breakfast. Without much appetite, I ate a half-portion of Miss Theresa's huge cinnamon rolls. Sam's appetite remained as healthy as usual, so I left him in the kitchen devouring the rest of mine along with his own.

With the door to my room open, I did some stretches like I'd do before a track meet. Sam poked his head in.

"What good will those exercises do? Shouldn't you be stretching your mouth?" He laughed, and I threw a slipper at him.

At church, I poked Sam and signed, "Pray for success today."

He gave me the thumbs-up sign.

After church, we had lunch at home as a family. Miss Theresa responded with excited approval when Sam told her and Mr. Tony that he was taking me with him to visit Levi.

"I'm so glad. You haven't gone over there in quite a while. It's good for Wendy to get to know your friends better too. I hope you both have fun." Her animated voice reached a high pitch.

Sam nodded. To me, he had deception written all over his face.

"Sam, be sure to tell everyone hello for your dad and me." She dove into her salad.

I smiled and hoped my intentions for the trip didn't leak from the pores on my face.

We arrived in front of Levi and Dev's house after a half-hour drive, my right knee pumping up and down.

"Don't be nervous." Sam killed the engine. "This can't be any worse than what happened at the center." He smirked.

I laughed, and my tension released somewhat.

At the door, I reached for the doorbell and then dropped my hand. Silly. We didn't want Dev to answer the door, and Levi wouldn't hear the bell.

Sam chuckled.

I slapped his arm playfully. "Okay, I know. I remembered," I signed, trying to be quiet. "It's not nice to make fun of the hearing," I mouthed and then grinned.

Sam returned the grin. "I texted Levi when we left.

He's watching for us."

Levi must've seen us because he opened the door. He welcomed us and signed, "Come in. Stay near the door."

He continued signing to Sam, which Sam translated to me in a low voice. "Dev doesn't know. I was afraid if she found out, she'd leave and be in more trouble with our parents."

Such a good brother.

We walked further inside, and Levi shut the door. Loudly, but not as loudly as Sam would have.

"Who's there?" Dev called from above us and then bounded down the stairs in bare feet wearing a wrinkled maxi dress that shouted she'd slept in it. She halted abruptly when she came face to face with Sam and me. Her eyes shifted between our faces. "What are you two doing here?" Her complexion drab, she stared at us without emotion.

I couldn't read Sam's face. I swallowed a lump in my throat.

Levi signed and Sam interpreted for me, even though I got it, "They've been thinking about you and wondering how you are, so they came for a visit."

Dev's face still held no expression. "I didn't need you to do this. Levi took a big chance letting you come here while our parents aren't home."

No one responded to her.

Levi slapped his hands together, startling me, and

then signed, "Need something to drink?"

Sam and I followed him into the kitchen. With my eyes open wide but mouth closed, I glanced from Levi to Sam. Levi acted every bit of normal, calmly preparing colas for us. Sam's face had flushed like he wasn't sure if this was going well. I knew it wasn't.

Levi gently signed close to Sam and me, "Dev takes time to adjust to anything new. Wait. We'll see."

We sat on counter stools with our glasses in front of us. I opened my mouth to start some casual conversation, just to break the silence. Then I remembered that would be rather ridiculous unless I wanted to listen to myself talk and have Sam read my lips.

As we sipped our drinks, Dev came in and fixed herself a cola. I caught her eye and attempted a smile. She cast a furtive glance my way and made one of those non-smiles, raising her lips from the chin instead of turning up the corners.

She stood still, holding her glass. With a flip of her head, she indicated I follow her. "Let's go to my room."

Levi and Sam grinned at each other and then at me. I hurried upstairs after Dev.

"I like your room." Light and bright, a pale yellow covered the walls. I immediately headed to one of the dormer windows for a bird-eye view of treetops and the gardens below them.

"Thanks. It's a good place for writing."

I turned from the window. "Do you like to write?"

128

"Mm-hmm." She stood at a cluttered desk and avoided my gaze.

"So do I. So far I've written only a short story." Other than papers for school, which I'd rather not think about.

She straightened some papers on the desk and said softly, "I write poetry."

High on the wall above her head, a quote stretched from corner to corner. Nicely done in calligraphy.

"Then I grasped the meaning of the greatest secret that human poetry and human thought and belief have to impart: The salvation of man is through love and in love." -Viktor E. Frankl

This wasn't about spiritual salvation but something else. Mortal existence. Humans couldn't live without love. I didn't recognize the author's name, but he must've experienced pain in his life. Her quote choice confirmed for me that Dev had the soul of a poet. Who would've thought?

I inched toward her, much like the approach I used for a frightened dog in need of help. My voice took the same kind of tone. "I love to read poetry but don't know how to write it. Maybe someday we can read each other's work."

"Maybe." She plopped onto her bed and looked me in the eye for the first time since entering her room. "But I know you didn't come here to talk about writing."

"No, I didn't. May I sit?"

"Sure. Pick a chair." Her voice welcomed me, but she still didn't smile.

I chose a comfy upholstered club chair. We stared at each other for a moment. I'd have to start the conversation. I looked down at my hands as I drew from the dialogue I'd written and memorized.

"We seem to have a lot in common. When my mom and dad divorced, I was sure my dad didn't love me." I looked up, and Dev's eyes were fixed on my face. With that encouragement, I kept going.

"He was an alcoholic, and I didn't receive the time and attention I thought all the other kids got from their fathers. Then I found out differently."

"Differently how?" She grabbed one of her pillows and hugged it.

"I learned about a lot of kids who had problems with their parents, some worse than I did. Fortunately, Dad started going to AA and became a better father than the one he'd been before."

She stared down at the pillow.

If one of her parents had a serious personal problem, wouldn't Levi have confided that to Sam? Hopefully, the only problem for Dev concerned her adoption. "I guess you've talked to your mom and dad about what happened the other day."

"Yeah, they kind of forced me to. They wanted to know why I didn't do the job I was sent there to do. So I told them I was tired of tagging along with Levi for everything, him making decisions for both of us based on what he liked, and my opinion not counting for anything."

"What did they say?" I relaxed into the chair and leaned an elbow on its arm.

"Typical parent stuff. Like, I haven't earned the right to make my own decisions. Levi sets a good example. Blah, blah, blah."

"Did you tell them why it bothers you so much that you only get to do what Levi chooses?" Did I sound like a psychologist, or what? Maybe I'd found my calling.

She took a deep breath and let it out. "I told them I didn't think they value me as much as they value him. Because he's their real son and behaves like a good Jewish boy. That I didn't think they love me as much as they do Levi because I'm adopted. They got really upset and denied it, of course." She squeezed the pillow closer to her chest.

"Maybe they just need some time to think about what you said."

"I wanted to say more. That I know I don't behave like a good Jewish daughter, but I'm only half Jewish. But then I'd have to tell them how I know I'm only half Jewish—that Bubbe had said my mom wasn't Jewish—and that was another reason I figured they don't love me as much. I didn't want to get Bubbe in trouble. I'm sure she wasn't supposed to say anything about my birth heritage in front of me."

"I understand being afraid of getting your

grandmother in trouble. But maybe you could explain to your parents that she didn't mean to let it slip out in front of you."

Dev heaved a loud sigh, letting her shoulders drop. "Look. I appreciate your concern about me. But if you came here to try to help, I don't know what you can do. I'm grounded for six weeks …"

Six weeks. A harsh penalty.

"… so I won't be able to see you or Sam. I wouldn't see you much longer anyway because you're leaving soon, but I wish I could see Sam. I shouldn't have messed up the volunteer thing."

No matter what, I could lessen her self-torture with at least one fact. "You should know that Sam and I are just friends. Very good friends, but still only friends."

She looked into my eyes. "Thanks for telling me. Either way, I'm sorry about the way I acted toward you. You were nice, and you tried to be my friend."

"Thanks for the apology. I'm okay now. Any time you want to be friends, we can be. I believe Sam thinks of you as a good friend too."

"Thanks. Sam will have to make up his own mind about whether to ask me out or not. Because he's friends with Levi, I might run into him again before the summer's over."

I cringed inside. The secret about her adoption had to come out soon for Sam's sake as well as hers. "I do have an idea that might help you open communication back up

132

with your parents and make you feel better too."

"What?" She narrowed her eyes.

"Why don't you ask your mom or dad who your birth parents are?"

Her eyes popped open wide. "No. Are you crazy? You should've seen them when I talked about being adopted."

I'd come prepared to say what I needed to say. It was now or never to force the idea out into the open where it could come alive and sprout legs. "If they would tell you who your birth parents are, you could ask if they think you're Jewish, half Jewish, or not really Jewish at all. You won't need to mention your Bubbe."

She shut her eyes and shook her head so hard it might come loose and spin across the room.

I talked faster and faster. "You could explain the thing about the Torah and ask if it would make them love you less. Wouldn't you rather know for sure?"

Her face red, Dev whacked the pillow against the bed. "You just don't get it. To them, the adoption case is closed."

She clamped her jaws and rattled her head, then her whole body, like in a violent shiver.

My voice rose to a pleading, high pitch. "You'd know better than me how to ask them, but the main thing is getting everyone to talk about it. They might understand you better and not be so mad at you."

She glared at me. "I said I can't. They'll flip if they

know I want to find my birth parents. I should never have confided in you that I wanted to search for them." She leapt off the bed and scowled.

"I'm sorry. I didn't mean to upset you." I scooted to the edge of my seat.

She folded her arms across her chest.

I stood up as gracefully as I could while trembling. "I really just wanted to help."

She ignored me.

I reached a hand toward her.

She stomped to the door and opened it. "Would you please go now?"

I walked out without looking back, and she slammed the door behind me.

With my eyes closed for a minute, blood pumped in my ears. What a spectacular mess I'd created from one already awful one.

Downstairs, I found Sam and Levi in the living room. They ejected themselves from lounge chairs and silently searched my face for an answer.

I signed, "I don't know. She's mad. It's complicated." Then I said to Sam, "I'll explain it to you on the way home, and you can explain it to Levi later. I'm done."

Sam signed to Levi that he'd talk to him about it later. I headed toward the car.

We pulled into a gas station on the way home, and I recounted my conversation with Dev to Sam. "Please don't say you tried to warn me. I feel bad enough as it is."

"I wouldn't say that to you. I knew it wouldn't be easy, but I understand that you wanted to help Dev. Maybe she'll understand eventually too."

"Maybe I wasn't the right person at the right time to talk to her about this." My stomach roiled. I eyed the button that would open my window.

"Do you feel like you did something wrong?"

I nodded. "I meddled in somebody else's business again, and this time it was somebody who's practically a stranger." I raised my hands and slapped my thighs with them.

Sam cut his eyes at me. He probably got what he needed to know from my body language. Shifting gears, he headed back onto the highway.

"Maybe it's pride that makes me do that kind of thing, and pride is a sin." I finger-spelled pride close to him and pointed to myself. Then I made the whole-word sign for *sin*.

He cast a sad look at me, his usually sunny eyes clouded over.

"I'm so clever I can solve everyone's problems." I mocked myself and shook my head.

He should get sarcasm. He's used it well himself.

"I feel like an idiot." My voice was tiny to match my insignificant feeling of worth.

"You know what Grandma Ana would say to you? She used to say it to my dad a lot." He glanced at me.

"No. What?" Hearing words of wisdom from Mrs. V, even indirectly, might help.

"Sometimes God uses a sinner to do His work."

Cynthia T. Toney

Chapter 14

I had to believe I'd done the right thing by talking with Dev about her adoption. No one else had stepped up to help her because they were sworn to secrecy. But after Sam and I returned home, my conversation with Dev replayed in my mind until I had to pray and beg God to please make it stop.

He sent Sam to the rescue.

"I have just the thing to clear our heads." Sam leaned through my doorway. "Change into some comfortable clothes and meet me in the garage."

"Where are your parents and Sarah?"

"They went shopping. We're on our own."

I changed into jeans and sneakers, ready for just about anything except cleaning the dirty garage.

When I caught up with him, he wore a knit hoodie covered in so many paint stains it was hard to determine its original color. He'd taken a bicycle off a wall rack and was wiping it down with a damp rag.

Cynthia T. Toney

"Which one do you want?" He grinned.

I pointed to a red bike. "You remembered I like to ride."

"Of course. But I would've made you ride with me anyway."

I laughed. He knew how to cheer me up.

He finished wiping down the bikes then put air in the tires. I teased him about his hoodie-of-many-colors, and we jumped onto our bikes and raced down the driveway. Laughing, we headed to downtown Anchorage.

The city was like nothing I'd seen before. Flowers in garden beds and hanging baskets bloomed outside every business. All over there were mounds of flowers. Mountains formed a backdrop, their peaks piercing the sky, their snowcaps glinting. The warm sun shone bright while a cool breeze blew strands of my hair into my eyes and mouth.

Sam came up beside me and laughed. "Are you cold?"

"No, the weather feels wonderful. So much better than Louisiana in June." Of course, I wore the pink sweater Mrs. V gave me for my birthday. I'd slipped it on at the last minute before we left.

We biked leisurely, with me in line behind Sam. Then side-by-side we traveled part of a trail and through a park with ducks and geese meandering around people seated in the grass. Sam raced ahead of me, and then I sped up and surged ahead. We continued for a few

139

minutes, laughing out loud, with kids turning and waving at us. Eventually we made our way back into downtown. My legs ached, but it was a good ache. Better than an aching heart.

Sam pulled alongside me. "Let's find a place to stop."

I nodded, and we soon parked the bikes outside a coffee shop. I found an outdoor table, and Sam ordered our drinks.

We settled into our chairs and sipped flavored coffees without speaking for a few minutes.

I sighed. "If I lived here, I'd feel closer to God all the time."

He looked to the mountains and sky and smiled. "I do. And I don't feel a lot of stress here."

"I'd like to return as often as possible."

"I'd like you to." He raised his cup. "To the future."

"To the future." I raised my cup and smiled.

Enjoying a pleasant tiredness from the bike ride, I sat on my bed that evening after dinner to further study ASL. I'd been depending on Sam to help me communicate with Levi, but he wasn't always around. If I was alone the next time I saw Levi and asked him about Dev, my signing needed to be as precise as I could make it. And if he answered me, I wanted to understand him perfectly.

Sam had begun to leave his door open much of the time when he was in his bedroom. Just the invitation I needed.

I stood in his doorway with the ASL book behind my back and leaned sideways against the door's frame. Unaware of my presence, he sorted and arranged his art supplies on a small table next to his easel.

He glanced up and noticed me. "It's not nice to sneak up on the deaf. How long have you been standing there?"

"Sorry." I stood up straight. "It was nice to watch you. You seemed to enjoy it all."

"I like knowing where all my tools are. It makes the work easier. I don't want to substitute a tool because I can't find the right one." He dusted his hands. "What are you up to?"

"Studying ASL." Carrying the book, I walked a few steps in, though not invited.

"When you're back home, we could Skype in ASL. If you're skilled enough by then."

"I hope to be. Would you let me practice with you?"

"When?"

"Right now."

He rubbed his chin. "Hmm. I will if you'll model for me."

I touched my warming cheek. "Oh. I'm flattered."

He chuckled. "If you choose to be."

My mouth dropped open. "Huh?"

"Just kidding. Come on." He positioned a hard, wooden chair several feet from the easel.

I tried to peek around the easel at his drawing pad.

He turned it before I could see anything. "No way."

"Are you working on the same drawing as before?"

"Yes. I need you to help me get the pose and the anatomy right."

"Anatomy? I'm not taking off my clothes."

"Don't be ridiculous. Nobody's asking you to do that."

"Oh. Then okay." I sat on the chair and placed my book on the floor.

"It would help if I could see your arms, though."

I removed my cardigan sweater and rolled up the sleeves of my tee-shirt to the shoulders.

He took the sweater from my lap and tossed it on his bed. "So, sit still a few minutes for me while I sketch. When I'm ready to put in detail, I'll let you know and you can relax and practice signing to me. We could try working like that."

"That sounds good." I wiggled on the chair and swiped hair from my eyes.

"Angle your body a little to the left. Now turn your head to the right a little. The shoulder …" He walked over and placed his hands on my shoulders. With a gentle touch, he positioned first one and then the other.

The sensation from his warm hands on my skin created goosebumps.

"Are you cold?" He frowned, his eyes worried.

"No." Only pleasantly surprised.

He stepped back and studied his subject. Then he came up to me again and brought my hair forward on one

142

side.

"May I breathe?" I meant as the model. I'd already stopped breathing when he touched me.

"Of course, but try not to move. Can you stay that way a few minutes? Let me know if you're uncomfortable."

"I'm fine for now." In reality, my neck stiffened and my upper lip perspired.

His gaze roved over my form as he stroked charcoal on paper. What kind of drawing was he doing that required me to model my arms?

It had better not be a nude.

He straightened his back and dropped his arm to his side. "Need a break?"

"Yes." I stretched my neck.

"Try to remember how I posed you." He laid the piece of charcoal on the table and cracked his knuckles.

"I'll try." I stood and finished stretching my arms and back.

"Now you can sign to me. Come closer." He picked up the charcoal and continued working.

How was he going to follow what I said? Anyway, I started signing the whole words I knew while I spoke.

"When did you start drawing? Do you see a finished drawing in your head before you start it? Why do you like to work in charcoal?"

He understood each question and signed back the answers with hardly a second's break in his drawing.

143

"When I was twelve, yes, and because I can affect the mood of the image better."

"How do you do that?" I signed.

He had barely even looked at me, his charcoal stick constantly moving over the paper.

"Do what?"

"Work and communicate at the same time."

"I've always done that. Haven't you?" He looked at me around the edge of his drawing and grinned.

Since I'd known him, he'd had that way of making the two of us seem more alike than different. Not a deaf boy and a hearing girl, but two friends who understood each other like any two good friends would.

Signing was always easier when you had something real to talk about.

When I got back to my room, I remembered that I'd forgotten something. I'd forgotten all about Dev and wanting to communicate with Levi about her, the reason I'd gone to Sam's room in the first place.

Monday, Levi walked straight up to me at the center without Sam anywhere around. "Dev wants your phone number," he signed.

I raised my eyebrows. "True?" I signed using a whole-word sign instead of finger-spelling "really."

He grinned and signed the same back to me.

"OK," I signed.

He signed, "She's a puzzle."

I laughed and nodded.

He handed me his phone. I punched in my number under my name, which he'd entered as a contact.

All day I waited for Dev to call. Not really waited because I stayed busy. Without Dev there, an older volunteer—older meaning a high school senior girl—worked with me. We got more done together than I ever did with Dev.

I missed her anyway.

After dinner and clean-up, my phone had a text message from Dev. I'd expected to hear the ringtone from a call and hadn't bothered to check messages for a while.

I sat on my bed.

Dev: YOU WANTED TO SEE SOME OF MY POETRY. I FINISHED THIS POEM TODAY. OPEN THE ATTACHMENT.

I opened it, and the first words took my breath away.

The Petitioner

I am loathe to tempt my fate
Lived within these walls sublime;
For the deeds of others late
Formed the choice before my time.

As the stewards labor long

In my interest for my needs,
Do they hear my mournful song
And my heart that often bleeds?

If I am to find my place
Let no fact remain unseen;
Not the past should be erased
If the future it shall mean.

Take the home where I shall dwell
If it pleases to endure
Make it build the life I tell
Help me grow both strong and sure.

Dev's sadness drew a shaky breath from me, and I yanked a tissue from the nearby box. If ever a poem could convey her emotional needs, this one had.

I texted back as I wiped my eyes: IT'S BEAUTIFUL. VERY TOUCHING. I FEEL YOUR EMOTIONS COMING THROUGH.

Did I dare suggest she show it to her parents?

Dev: THANK YOU. I'M GLAD YOU LIKE IT.

Me: I UNDERSTAND YOU BETTER NOW.

It took a minute for her response.

Dev: IT MEANS A LOT TO ME THAT YOU TRY TO UNDERSTAND ME. I KNOW IT'S NOT EASY.

Me: YOU DESERVE IT.

Another minute passed. Was the conversation over?

DEV: SEND ME SOMETHING OF YOURS TO HELP ME UNDERSTAND YOU BETTER.

ME: I'LL WORK ON IT. I DON'T HAVE ANYTHING HERE.

DEV: OK

ME: DEV?

DEV: YES?

I gritted my teeth. It wasn't too late to change my mind, but …

ME: HAVE YOU THOUGHT ABOUT SHOWING YOUR POEM TO ANYONE ELSE?

No answer after two minutes. *Ugh.* I pushed too far too soon. She was gone.

I sighed and stood up, tossing my phone on the bed. May as well do something constructive. My pajama bottoms and tee-shirts lay in a dirty pile in the corner of the room. I scooped up the clothes and carried them to the laundry room to wash.

I returned in a few minutes to find Dev's final response.

SORRY, BUT I NEED TO GO. GOOD NIGHT.

She'd crept so close to me, and I'd scared her off. Again.

God, please let Dev see that showing her parents the poem might help her. If You think so. Amen.

It seemed like her best chance to me.

Chapter 15

The next morning after arriving at the center, I split off from Sam right away and headed to see the wolf pups. I'd been missing them and wanted a quick visit before checking the schedule.

Dev texted me again. What a coincidence that I was there with the pups.

DEV: I'VE BEEN THINKING ABOUT PUAH. HOW IS SHE?

ME: GETTING BIG AND STRONG! ALL THE PUPS ARE BEAUTIFUL, BUT ESPECIALLY PUAH. I'M WITH THEM NOW.

DEV: I MISS HER. I'M SORRY I DIDN'T SPEND MORE TIME WITH HER WHILE I WAS AT THE CENTER.

ME: AWW. WOULD YOU LIKE SOME PICS OF HER?

DEV: THAT WOULD BE GREAT. THANKS.

ME: ACHIRAM AND PUAH PLAY SO CUTE TOGETHER. I WISH YOU COULD SEE THEM. I'LL TRY TO GET A VIDEO TOO.

DEV: THANK YOU. KISS PUAH FOR ME.

ME: I WILL. HOW ARE YOU DOING?

DEV: FINE. I HAVE A LOT OF CHORES TO DO WHILE I'M

HOME. BUT I'M WRITING MORE POETRY.

ME: THE TIME WILL GO BY FAST. I'M GLAD YOU'RE WRITING. I HAVEN'T WRITTEN ANYTHING SO FAR THIS SUMMER.

DEV: I'M SORRY I CUT YOU OFF YESTERDAY.

ME: THAT'S OK. YOU MUST HAVE A LOT ON YOUR MIND.

I took some quick photos of the pups wrestling with one another and then checked my phone again.

DEV: I DECIDED I'LL SHOW THAT POEM TO MY PARENTS.

A jolt went through my temporal lobe. *Thank you, God.*

I took in a chestful of air through my smile.

ME: THAT'S A GOOD IDEA.

If I understood Dev better from reading her poem, shouldn't her parents?

My departure date loomed, so I made a little extra time for the wolf pups.

"I'll miss you when I go home, Achiram. I wish I didn't have to leave you." I snuggled with the pup, so lively I had trouble holding onto him and my phone at the same time.

So much for taking a selfie.

"Would you like a photo with him?" The older volunteer girl who'd worked with me after Dev left was a hard worker but pretty quiet. She had a friendly smile, though.

"Oh, yes. Thank you." I handed her the phone.

Achiram pounced on me. The surprise knocked me off balance. Soon he had me on the ground laughing.

"I got some good ones." The girl held my phone and scrolled through the images. "Want any with the other pups?"

"That would be nice." I stood up, and Achiram left to chase another pup. I reached for Puah and drew her close, squatting on the ground next to her.

"Somebody asked me to give you kisses for her." I smooched the top of Puah's head. Puah was more docile than Achiram. She let me bend on one knee next to her and hold her steady with one hand while the other girl got the shot. Dev was going to love having a photo of her standing tall and looking so regal.

I went to each of the other pups and said their names as I stroked their coats. Achiram and Puah tried to climb onto my back. I stood up, and all the pups started teasing one another, shoving, pouncing, and nipping.

How could I not shoot a video of that?

Their little yips and yowls had the other girl and me laughing until we got hiccups.

How could I be so happy and so sad about the pups at the same time? Or back and forth? Sad each time I saw

150

them because they didn't have a mother, happy the center gave them safety, and I got to help care for them. Sad that I had to leave them soon and not see them grow up, but happy they would grow up big and strong and hopefully return to the wild someday.

I rested against a tree and closed my eyes, using my other senses to absorb the sounds, smells, and textures surrounding me. The Conservation Center had become both a second home and a place of learning as much as any school could've been.

At seven the next morning, my phone rang in my pocket as I poured a glass of orange juice for breakfast.

My heart jumped. Why would anyone call me this early? On a holiday. The Fourth of July, Independence Day. Disaster at home? Sickness? Accident?

I wrestled the phone out of my pocket.

Dev.

"Hello?"

"Wendy, I gave the poem to my parents late last night and asked them to read it." She spoke in breathless spurts.

Thank you, God. "That's great, Dev. You sound excited."

"I am. They were sitting in the living room when I

handed it to my mother on the sofa. I told her it was a poem expressing my feelings, and I asked her if they would both read it. When I walked away and glanced back, my father had gotten up from his chair and was sitting next to her."

"That's hopeful. How do you feel?"

"I feel better already, just knowing they cared enough to read it. No matter what happens now, at least I can say I tried to get them to understand me."

"I'm glad you feel good about taking that step. I always feel better when I get my worries out in the open."

"Thank you for not giving up on trying to help me."

"You're welcome. I'm praying everything works out great for you."

"Thanks for your prayers. No matter what, I'm glad I gave them the poem."

"Do you think they'll talk to you this morning?"

"I don't know. I'm not worried they haven't said anything to me yet and might not talk to me today. They usually take a long time to think about things."

I smiled. Dev was like them in that way. She probably didn't even realize it. In what other ways might she be similar to her adopted parents?

I rushed to Sam's room to tell him about Dev's poem and how she'd given it to her parents.

He sat on his bed, tying the laces on his shoes. "You amaze me."

In a good or bad way? I tapped his shoulder, and he

152

looked up. "What do you mean?"

"When you decide to help someone, you usually think of an unusual way to do it." He flexed his feet and then stood up.

"You mean the poem? Dev wrote it, and it fit the situation." Still, his words sent a warm wave through me.

"Well, not just anyone would've asked to read her poetry or thought to tell her to show it to her parents. And even if they thought it, they might not have actually encouraged her."

I smiled. With elbows bent and hands closed, I twisted my torso a few times in a stationary dance. "That's nice of you to say."

"If I ever need help, I want you on my team." He grinned.

"You got it."

We walked into the hall.

Halfway down the hall, he grabbed my arm and looked me in the eyes. "Now we wait and see what happens, okay? About the poem, I mean. See if her parents tell her any more about the adoption."

"Right ..." I shifted my eyes. It all depended.

We continued to the kitchen.

He filled a glass with water from the dispenser on the refrigerator door. "You'll wait, won't you? You won't push." He guzzled the water and set the glass on the counter.

"I'll try to be patient. I promise. But you know how

hard that is for me."

"I know. In the meantime, let's do something today I've been thinking about."

"What's that?" I retrieved my orange juice and took a swallow.

"Let's go see Grandma. We don't need to wait for my mom or dad to take you. I can do it."

My heart lifted. "That's a great idea. Your mom and dad try to arrange the time for me to go, but I know it's easier for them to see her during the day when we're at the center."

"That's what I was thinking, so I asked if we could go without them." He selected a cereal bowl out of the cabinet.

"We should spend more time with Mrs. V anyway. Just the two of us."

"No." He reached into the pantry and grabbed a box of cereal.

"No?" I puzzled.

"Three of us. You, me, and Sarah." He filled his bowl as he talked. "I think it would be nice for Grandma to see all of her grandchildren at once."

My heart flipped. He truly understood how I felt about Mrs.V. I reached over and placed my hand on his shoulder and rubbed it. "You do know how important she is to me."

His voice was soft but grainy. "Yeah, I do. I always have."

Did Mrs. V still understand how much we all still loved her?

He read my mind. "Whether she remembers us or not, let's just be there with her."

"I agree. And I'm glad Sarah will go with us. She hasn't spent much time with her grandma since I've been here. I haven't spent much time with Sarah, either, and I want her to know I like her a lot."

"She knows. But just in case someone needs to tell you—she's crazy about you."

"Aww, how sweet."

"She really wants a sister."

"I'll try to be one for her today."

Chapter 16

Before noon, I showered and then helped Miss Theresa by setting the table for our holiday meal of burgers and turkey hot dogs Mr. Tony had grilled. I arranged some miniature American flags in a vase for a centerpiece and set out blue napkins and red dishes. Sarah mixed the potato salad.

After we sat down and prayed with the adults, Sam, Sarah, and I ate quickly.

"Sorry for gobbling my food, Miss Theresa." I took a last drink of water and picked up my plate to carry it to the sink.

She and Mr. Tony smiled at each other. "That's all right. We can tell all of you are excited to visit Ana on your own."

After Sarah and I rinsed our dishes and placed them in the dishwasher, I invited her to come to my room like I'd do if I were her big sister. She followed me.

"Sarah, what do you want to wear for the visit with

156

Grandma tonight?"

"I don't know." She looked down at her faded blue jeans. "I haven't thought about it."

"Would you like to try to coordinate what we wear or try to dress alike?"

"Yes."

"Okay. Should we start with jeans? That would be easy."

She nodded.

"Let's look at what colors we have in tops, then." I opened my closet and chest of drawers so we could browse.

"This is so pretty." She fingered the sleeve of light blue knit top embellished with beads.

"Thank you. That's my newest dressy top. Do you have anything that color? So we could match."

"No. I have something darker blue than that."

"Maybe we should start with your closet instead of mine."

She laughed. "That might be easier."

Sarah and I decided on red tops. She chose a short-sleeved knit top, and I suggested her white denim jacket over it. I put on a long-sleeved red shirt with a collar.

"Wait a minute." She left and returned with a white belt. "Mom said we could borrow this."

I tucked the front part of my shirt into my jeans and pulled the braided belt through the loops. "Now we're both dressed in red, white, and blue."

We approved of ourselves in a mirror and then met Sam in the kitchen.

He scowled at Sarah and me. "I feel underdressed." With two fingers of one hand, he pulled his standard grey tee-shirt away from his body.

Sarah slapped the air. "You look fine." She turned her back to him and said, "Who cares what he wears?"

I stifled a giggle, signing and speaking to Sam. "Feel free to change into a red tee-shirt." I wiggled my eyebrows.

"No way am I dressing like a triplet." He snorted.

"That's what I figured." Sarah giggled as she hooked an arm around mine.

All three of us headed to Sam's car.

The lobby of The Haven harbored a hospital smell when Sam, Sarah, and I passed through its doors. No one had tried to disguise it with a more pleasant scent like before. Even the red, white, and blue flower arrangement on the front desk didn't help the aroma. Or cheer the residents in the lobby.

Each visit, I'd dreaded the day when Mrs. V would be one of the old people sitting alone and sad in a wheelchair, unaware of her surroundings.

That day had come. Sam squeezed my left hand, and

I squeezed Sarah's hand with my right one.

A female caregiver pushed a man in a wheelchair and parked him next to Mrs. V. The caregiver started talking to both of them as we approached. They didn't speak to each other.

"Oh, hello," the caregiver said when she noticed us.

"Hi. We're Mrs. Villaturo's grandchildren," Sam said.

I warmed inside.

"I recognize you. I'm Betty." Her lips formed a small, tender smile.

Mrs. V's eyes held no light.

Sarah tightened her grip on me. "Is Grandma all right?" Her face flushed and her brow wrinkled.

Betty's eyes met mine. "Ana hasn't wanted to eat or talk today. I thought seeing her friend, Mr. Gomez, would spark something. Sometimes just being in the lobby and seeing other people helps."

"Is it helping?" I asked. Mrs. V's eyes and body language showed no sign of recognition. Of us, Mr. Gomez, or her surroundings.

"I'm afraid not. I was about to take her back to her apartment to see if I could get her to eat something. Would you like to join us?"

We all nodded. But it was sad that we had to leave poor Mr. Gomez alone in the lobby, staring straight ahead.

In Mrs. V's tiny kitchen, Betty parked Mrs. V's

wheelchair and sat in one of the chairs at the small eating table. A tray containing meager spoonfuls of food lay on the table.

"Doesn't she usually eat in the dining room?" I sat in one of the three chairs.

Sarah took the other chair, and Sam stood nearby.

Betty pressed her lips together. "She had been eating there until this week. We had to start feeding her when she didn't seem to know what to do with her food. She played with it and disturbed some of the other residents at her table. So we started bringing her meals to her." Betty scooped a little of what looked like mashed potatoes onto a fork and brought it to Mrs. V's lips.

Mrs. V took it in and then spit it out.

"Isn't she hungry?" Sarah's voice trembled.

"When is the last time she ate?" Sam's eyebrows drew together.

Betty sighed. "She hasn't eaten today. As the disease progresses, Alzheimer's victims don't taste what we put in their mouths. There's no incentive to eat if something doesn't taste good."

I signed to Sam to explain as best I could in case he didn't catch all of Betty's explanation. Sarah seemed too distraught to help communicate.

"May I try to feed her?" I reached across the corner of the little table and touched Mrs. V's arm. Not so long ago, she'd made me a scrambled egg sandwich and sat across from me in her kitchen in Louisiana, watching me eat it.

"Sure. Just try a little at a time."

The mashed green peas might have more flavor than the potatoes. I scooped some onto a spoon. Mrs. V seemed to look at my shirt.

"You chose a good color to wear. She often notices things that are red."

Mrs. V looked into my eyes, boring into them, as though seeking something she couldn't name. My head began to hurt.

I touched the spoon to her lips. She accepted the food and tried to swallow. Part of it must've gone down, but much of it didn't. I cleaned her face and the front of her clothes.

"The swallow reflex doesn't work as well either," Betty said.

Tears filled Sarah's eyes as she watched her grandmother try to eat.

After a few more tries of partial success, no mashed peas were left on the tray. Relieved Mrs. V had eaten for me, I relinquished the task of feeding to Betty. My heart ached. I might never feel like eating again, because someone I loved couldn't.

One look at Sarah's face told me she needed me. I coaxed her into the living room. We sat on the sofa, and I wrapped my arm around her.

"I thought it would make her feel happy to see us. I didn't know she would be like this," Sarah whispered.

"I feel sad seeing your grandma like this too. But I think deep down inside she's glad you came, and she knows you care about her." I stroked her hair. Sarah should hear comforting words at twelve years old, not medical facts.

I left Sarah in the living room and retraced the few steps to the kitchen. "Miss Betty, what do you usually offer Ana for breakfast?"

"Something easy to eat like cream of wheat or oatmeal. Usually with applesauce."

Sam made a face.

"If you could make a special request for us, could you ask the cook to make her some soft scrambled eggs?"

"I'll try." Betty smiled, and I believed her.

"It used to be her favorite breakfast." I choked out the words as my chin quivered.

Sam, Sarah, and I said goodbye to our grandmother and rode home in silence. I sat in the back seat with Sarah, and she leaned her head on my shoulder.

When we returned home, Sarah went straight to the living room and crawled up on the sofa next to her mom. Miss Theresa cuddled her.

I got a drink of water in the kitchen. "Sam, can we go in the back yard?"

"Sure." Sam turned on the porch light.

We went outside and settled into a teak bench.

I rubbed my eyes and sniffed. "Your parents said Mrs. V was getting worse. I just didn't think she would be that bad."

"Dad goes to see her almost every day if his work allows. Mom does too, or she asks Dad. I guess they see her change a little at a time, but we saw it all of a sudden." Sam's voice lowered. "But there's nothing they or anyone can do."

My shoulders sagged. "I almost started crying tonight. But I wanted to stay strong for Sarah."

He wrapped an arm around my shoulders. "I know what you mean. I wanted to stay strong for both of you."

We looked into each other's eyes, tears welling up for both of us.

Chapter 17

That night, I prayed for good news. From anyone. I believed in happy endings, and all of us needed one.

If Mrs. V and Sam's family couldn't have a happy ending, then what about Dev and her family? Alice and Jerome? Jennifer? David and me?

My phone startled me out of my reverie.

Dev.

Hopefully she wouldn't be crying. For both our sakes.

If she cried, I might cry too. I was continuously on the verge because of Mrs. V, and the smallest trigger could get me started. Bad news from Dev might push me over the edge.

"Hi, Dev." I kept my voice even.

"Oh, Wendy. You're not going to believe what happened."

I slumped. Oh, no. She was crying.

I swallowed and toughened up. "Whatever it is,

you'll be okay," I stated calmly. That's what a friend was supposed to say, wasn't it?

"I'll definitely be okay. My mom and dad loved my poem. Thank you for pushing me to give it to them."

My joy was like a little hummingbird's when it finds the right flower. "I'm so happy for you. And you're welcome."

"They said they understood me better after reading it, just like you did. They asked me questions about my worries over being adopted."

"They wanted you to talk about it? That's great, Dev."

"I said I needed their help and needed them to know why I've been acting like I have."

"That was a good way to put it." If only all of my friends had gone to their parents in time.

Her voice calmed and lowered an octave. "I finally asked them about my birth parents."

I took a deep breath. This was it. "Good for you. What did you say?"

"I told them I needed to know who they are. Knowing wouldn't make me love them any less, but it would help me figure out who I am and why I don't feel like I fit in."

Smart girl. "What did they say?"

"They told me." Her voice shook. "They told me everything." She drew the words out and then grew quiet.

I held my breath. "Everything" needed to be the

whole truth, the absolute truth.

The other end of the conversation remained silent.

"You can tell me if you like." But I hadn't figured how I would react if the truth came out and Dev shared it with me.

In a tiny voice, she said, "I'm embarrassed."

I never wanted that. She had to see how much better knowing the truth was for her in the long run. "No matter who they were, you don't need to be embarrassed."

"I'm not so sure. They were a teenage couple. And my mother was... Sam's aunt."

"Sam's aunt?" I took a deep breath and blew it out through my mouth. I'd let Dev draw her own conclusions about my knowledge—or Sam's—of the facts of her birth.

"What Bubbe told me was true—my mother wasn't Jewish. But I had no idea she could've been so close, I mean related to someone I already knew. Sam, of all people. Now I feel so weird because of the feelings I had about him."

"I'd feel weird too. But weird circumstances usually surround adoptions, don't you think?"

"I guess."

I had to move this along to the positive aspects. "Did you and your parents talk about your being half Jewish?"

Her voice brightened. "They said it didn't matter. It really didn't matter. And I believe them. I am wholly their daughter and wholly Jewish in their eyes and hearts."

"This is so wonderful, Dev. The power of prayer, right? Did they say what happened to your birth parents after they adopted you?" I bit my lip. If she knew, I prayed she'd handle it well.

She sighed. "It's not good. They're dead. Killed." Her voice caught. "In a car accident."

I gripped my phone tighter. "I'm so sorry they died. And sorry you won't get to meet them. You were looking forward to that."

She cleared her throat. "But the most horrible part is that Sam is my cousin, and I've been trying to get him to go out with me. You've seen how I acted. I was over the top, even for a boy who wasn't my cousin. I'd be mortified if my parents ever find out about it."

"I think you're forgetting something. Sam is a caring person. He wouldn't tell, and he wouldn't do anything to make you feel bad. And I don't think you need to feel ashamed about what you did before you found out he was your cousin."

"You're probably right about Sam. I want to believe that he can look at me in a new way. I really want to get to know him and his family better."

"I think the next person you should talk to is Sam."

The next day at the center, Dev and Sam texted with

each other, back and forth. Levi and I exchanged glances when we both happened to catch Sam rapid-fire punching into his phone.

"I know what's going on," Levi signed to me. "My parents told me."

"Me too," I signed. "From Dev."

"I'm glad they talk about it," he signed.

I nodded and signed "yes."

Levi watched Sam a moment longer. "They worked it out."

I'd gotten used to Levi picking up a lot of information by studying the body language of the hearing people around him, just like I did.

Levi signed some more, and I managed to keep up. "I think it was good Dev was stuck at home. Probably easier for her to text with Sam about everything instead of seeing and talking face to face." Of course, he signed only the important words, leaving the rest for me to fill in.

"I agree," I signed.

I caught up with Sam and Levi again at lunch. "How are things going?" I laid my food on the table and signed as I spoke. Then I sat down next to Sam and across from Levi.

"All good. I think Dev and I covered everything." Sam spoke to me as he signed for Levi.

"I hope so. Your phone needed a rest." I grinned and took a bite of my sandwich.

Sam continued signing for Levi and said to me, "She

was worried how I'd feel about her. Afraid I'd think badly of her and not want to have anything to do with her. I told her, *no way*."

"I'm glad you worked it out. I knew how bad she felt, and I said she should talk to you. I told her you were a nice guy."

Sam smiled. "Thanks. She apologized to me for the way she acted."

"And what did you say?"

"Not to worry."

"See? Nice guy."

Saturday morning, my mind was at peace and my body at rest. Dressed in my most comfortable leggings and a knit tunic, I relaxed in the bed, ending a text conversation with Alice.

"Family meeting!" Miss Theresa announced from one end of the hall to the other.

I leapt up and then froze near my open door.

"Wendy, come on. Family meeting." Sarah smiled and reached for my hand, but I gently pulled back.

"I don't know, Sarah. It might be about something I shouldn't hear." I grinned and whispered, "Maybe Sam's in trouble." In reality, the Villaturos deserved a private moment as a family once in a while without me around.

Sam joined us at my door. "Family meeting, Wendy." He extended his hand for mine.

I hesitated a second and looked at him and Sarah. Then I placed my palm on top of his. The three of us walked together to the dining room.

Already there, Mr. Tony spoke first. "Wendy, I don't blame you for looking rather confused, but all of us agreed you should attend this meeting. You've played a big part in this situation."

My heart and stomach collided with each other. They must've been angry with me for something. Did they know what I'd done with Dev? My hands shook as I pulled out a chair and sat down.

Miss Theresa's eyes softened, and she touched my arm. "You've gone pale. Don't worry. We're not upset with you."

I blinked a few times, and my breathing relaxed.

"Sam told me that Devorah asked her parents who her birth parents were, and they told her. He helped me understand that you persuaded her to ask them, but you did it out of concern for Dev." Miss Theresa raised her eyebrows as though she expected a response.

"Yes, ma'am. Dev reminded me of other people I've known who thought they weren't loved and who did drastic things to themselves because that's what they believed."

"Your mom shared with me some things that happened to your friends."

"They didn't understand how wonderful God had made them or how valuable they were. I didn't want that to happen to Dev."

"I know." Miss Theresa signed for Sam as she spoke to me. "Tony and I appreciate what a good friend you are. Dev is lucky to have you. We all are."

I squirmed from her praise. "Thank you, Miss Theresa."

"Honestly, I'm relieved not to have to keep my sister's secret any longer. I think under the circumstances, she would want Dev to know everything now. She wouldn't want Dev to feel like she doesn't belong anywhere because she doesn't know where she came from. I don't either. And if knowing about my sister helped Dev learn how much her adopted parents truly love her, then I want that too."

Sam hugged Miss Theresa. "Mom, I'm happy I finally have a cousin."

"Me too." Sarah bounced in her seat.

"I'm glad to be an aunt and finally be able to admit that to my niece."

Mr. Tony slapped both palms on top of the table. "Sounds like we need to plan a family reunion."

Miss Theresa kissed Mr. Tony's cheek.

He stood up and said, "Or since it would be the first time, would it be just a family 'union'?"

All of us burst out laughing.

Dev had gained much more than the confirmation of

her adopted parents' love. She secured an extended family that had been right under her nose her whole life.

Chapter 18

The Villaturos were hosting a Sunday cookout—a "union" of Sam's family and Dev's.

I'd vacuumed the living room and dusted the furniture while Miss Theresa baked a cake and Mr. Tony prepared food for cooking on the grill. Kosher, of course. Miss Theresa had consulted with Dev's parents on the menu. Whatever the Villaturos were not able to prepare themselves, they ordered from a Kosher deli.

Including bagels and lox.

"Can I help with the decorations?" Anything to get my mind off the delicious-smelling food.

Miss Theresa slapped a roll of streamer paper into my hand and hugged me. "We're making this a combination becoming-a-union party and going-away party because you'll be leaving us the day after tomorrow. So, let's do it up special."

Sam stood on a ladder hanging a banner in the foyer that read "Welcome" in letters printed on colorful foil squares. He stepped off the ladder and squinted one eye and then the other. "Is it straight?"

I viewed from across the room. "It looks good to me."

"Great." He picked up the ladder. "Help me with the other one."

"Why another one?"

"You'll see." He unwrapped the banner and held it up. It read "Farewell."

Sadness slammed my chest. I wasn't quite ready to say "Farewell." I winced, rubbed my eyes, and then folded my arms across my chest.

Sam read my body language. "It'll be okay. Let's just have fun today and not worry about tomorrow or the next day."

A friend who wasn't a worrier proved to be a good thing for a worrier like me. I nodded and forced a smile.

I draped ribbons of various colors on the dining room chandelier. Sarah laid out a tablecloth and china plates, napkins, and eating utensils on the table. When she finished, she asked me to check her work.

"It looks beautiful, Sarah." We hugged each other.

"I'm going to miss you. Don't forget me," she said in a small voice.

If only the Villaturos were going back to Louisiana with me. "I'll miss you too, and I'll never forget you. Plus, Sam said we could Skype. How's that?"

"That would be great."

174

I released my hold. "We'd better go get dressed for the party."

"Can we dress in matching colors again?"

"Why not? But let's hurry."

We chose black pants and yellow tops. Black for the special occasion and yellow for the brilliant Alaskan sun.

The doorbell rang, and I rushed to answer it, beating Sam and Sarah there. I didn't get the door swung all the way open before Dev leaped forward.

Eyes bright, she grabbed and hugged me. We twisted sideways, giggled, and nearly fell over.

She let go, and I regained my balance. She stayed between her parents and me. "Mom and Dad, this is my friend Wendy."

Little bubbles sprung up in my insides. Her friend.

I smiled at the adults, conservatively dressed in plain, dark clothing. Dev's father wore a beard. Both had warm smiles. "It's very nice to meet you. Please come in."

Levi signed, "Hello," and Sam signed back to him and the adults.

Dev and Sam exchanged glances and nods. Everything was okay. I took a deep breath of relief.

Sarah hung back until I said to the adults, "Do you remember Sam's sister, Sarah?"

"Hi, Sarah," Dev said.

"Oh, yes, of course. She's grown up," Dev's father said.

Sarah blushed and smiled. "Hello."

I closed the door. "Everyone else is outside in the back. Like the sign says, 'Welcome.'" I turned toward the kitchen.

Miss Theresa had entered the house without being noticed and stood as still as a statue between the living room and kitchen, her face flushed. All talk ceased.

Then, she slowly opened her arms.

Dev went to her. "Aunt Theresa." They clung to each other and sobbed.

Sam and I hung onto each other, and Sarah joined us.

Tears rolled down Miss Theresa's cheeks. "I've wanted so long to tell you how much you remind me of my sister," she said, her face pressed against the side of Dev's head.

"I'm so happy to be a part of your family."

Dev's mother held fingers to her lips and sniffed. Her father wipes his eyes with a handkerchief.

Levi and Sam were the only two people not crying. Guys.

"I can't wait to get to know you better, Aunt Theresa." Dev pulled back and smiled.

"Aww" rippled through the crowd.

"I can't either. We are now officially family." Miss Theresa hugged Dev's mother. Her father took Miss Theresa's hand between his.

Mr. Tony cleared his throat. "Anyone hungry?"

"Oh, yes," I blurted, and everyone laughed. For the first time in days, I had an appetite.

Sam extended a hand to Dev. "Shall we dine, cousin?"

She smiled and placed her hand in his.

That night, Sam and I sat side-by-side on my floor, leaning our backs against the bottom of the bed.

"Do you feel as weird as I do?" I laughed the kind of nervous laugh that says I-hope-you-won't-make-fun-of-me.

"Pretty weird." He turned toward me and took my hand, possibly the best hand hold ever. "Like the past five weeks have been a dream. When I wake up after you leave, it'll seem like you weren't really here. Tonight, I want to draw everything about our time together before I forget any of it."

"I hope you do. Will you send me a sketch? I framed the one you did of me and Mrs. V. It hangs on my bedroom wall."

"I'm flattered, and I'll send you something new." He kissed my temple.

Shivers ran down to my toes.

"Do you think we'll see each other again?" My eyes searched his. "Because I do."

"We will see each other again. Many times, I believe. And not just on Skype." He smiled and then squeezed my hand and looked down at it.

I looked too, and captured a memory of our hands held together.

He let go and stroked my hair. "It's just that, right now, this is all we can have. But it's good."

"It is good." I stared into his eyes, warm and bright like the sun.

The way Sam had acted on our date made sense. We were soon to be thousands of miles apart again.

I rested my head on his shoulder. He and I were both a little different at that moment from the way we were less than a year ago. If we met again at different times in the future, would we be different people each time?

Only God would know what that might mean until it happened.

My bags lay in the trunk of Mr. Tony's car parked at The Haven. Once again, I was saying goodbye to Mrs. V. Sam accompanied me.

In her apartment, a lunch tray containing only a spoonful of each food sat on the tiny kitchen table. Including soft-scrambled eggs like I'd suggested.

The caregiver Betty attempted to feed Mrs. V like a baby, just as I had done last time I was there. Mrs. V let the food drip or fall out of her mouth. Even the eggs didn't work.

"I'm sorry," Betty said. "She ate the eggs once, but that's all."

"Thank you for trying," I said.

Mrs. V's skin hung on her bones.

"I'll let you spend some time with her, and I'll try to feed her later." She wiped Mrs. V's mouth and chin with a napkin.

"Thank you." Mr. Tony rolled Mrs. V's wheelchair into the living room. I sat in a chair next to her. Sam and Tony sat opposite us, on the sofa.

I held up my wrist, toyed with the puppy charm on the new chain bracelet, and smiled at Mrs. V. Her face offered no expression.

I kissed her cheek. She gave no reaction. Did she feel anything regarding the charm or my kiss? Through reading about Alzheimer's, I'd learned feelings and memories are all jumbled up inside of her. From different times and places. Sometimes the person just can't sort them or get them out. How sad and frustrating that must be.

"We're going now, Mama." Mr. Tony walked over to her and stroked her shoulder and kissed the top of her head. "Wendy has to go back home to Louisiana."

Sam knelt in front of Mrs. V, his head on the same level as hers. "I love you, Grandma."

I held back tears and spoke to whoever might understand me, praying Mrs. V would. "I'll try to visit again next summer and see you." I couldn't not say it. If I said it, maybe I could make it come true, for her and for me. I leaned over, hugged her gently, and kissed her cheek.

Mr. Tony smiled weakly. Sam and I stood, and we headed for the door.

"You should prepare yourself," Mr. Tony said in a low voice as we walked out and into the hall, "in case she doesn't live until next summer."

My face must've reflected the sudden, sharp pain in my gut. He didn't need to tell me this goodbye would likely be the last. I already knew.

He quickly added, "But her caregivers say she might come around again. Sometimes they take a bad turn like this but then surprise everyone by regaining strength and appetite for a short while. She might even have some days when she remembers us."

I nodded silently. I wouldn't be there to see it.

Sam rubbed my back. "I'll keep in touch with you about her, like always."

I raised my eyes to Sam's face. His eyes were wet too.

Chapter 19

I boarded the plane to Seattle, thanking God for His beautiful creation that was Alaska. And the people I'd met. The opportunities I'd received. The time with Mrs. V and with Sam.

Soon, Sarah should find the gift I'd left for her, if she hadn't already. My light blue top she'd admired. She'd grow into it in no time. I would imagine her wearing it and remembering me. Maybe even see her wearing it on Skype.

I found my seat, and my phone notified me of a text as I sat down.

Sam: I DIDN'T GET TO FINISH THIS DRAWING WHILE YOU WERE HERE, BUT I PROMISE I'LL MAIL IT TO YOU AS SOON AS IT'S DONE.

The one from the easel? I smiled. Sam was good at keeping a secret until the right moment to spring it on me.

I enlarged and scanned through the image. One side had a lot of white space around some strong lines in charcoal. The other side looked complete, with shadows and highlights in the hair, loosely curled and falling over the shoulder. I wore the dress I had on the night we went out to eat at the Italian place.

He didn't need to work on it any further. Not for me. He'd captured me perfectly.

Me: THANK YOU SO MUCH. IT'S BEAUTIFUL, AND I LOVE IT JUST THE WAY IT IS.

It was me, a girl unfinished, waiting to be filled in by life. Still learning, seeking truth about myself and those around me.

God would show me how best to do both in the future. He'd guide me to completion.

The plane took off, and my window shrunk the majestic scenery smaller and smaller until the mountains and buildings resembled toys I'd left behind. I turned away as clouds covered them from view.

High in the air, I took a deep breath and chuckled. I'd wanted so badly this summer to forget the things that had caused me pain or sorrow.

I'd heard people say it's important to forget life's pain. Just shove the past to the back and look forward to the future. Why would anyone say that?

I no longer wanted to forget. If I put Mrs. V out of my mind—or David or the editing-for-hire incident—I wouldn't only forget the bad things. I'd lose the beautiful memories too. Like eating scrambled egg sandwiches with Mrs. V the summer after eighth grade, when I was

182

lonely for Jennifer. Laughing with David when we teased each other. The first time he kissed me—my first kiss ever. Getting to know Melissa while I helped her with her writing assignment. The real Melissa, not the stuck-up Stick. Someone I grew to like.

Leaving Louisiana behind didn't stop me from experiencing challenges. I'd faced struggles in Alaska too. But the struggles with Dev and Sam resulted in a new friendship with one and a stronger friendship with the other. Working with the wolf pups at the Conservation Center and having to leave them behind taught me how to cope with letting go of animals. That lesson would help me as I continued to foster rescued dogs back home. Maybe I wouldn't cry so hard each time I said goodbye to one of them.

So, maybe it was better to remember the things I'd shared with people and animals I'd cared about and who'd cared about me. Even if we couldn't stay together or if they couldn't love me back for long. Or remember me forever.

I pulled my notebook from my tote, conveniently stashed there because I had suspected I might want to write. I owed someone a poem, so I began.

For Dev.

Poem completed, I made my connecting flight to New Orleans for the second leg of the trip home.

I enjoyed a plastic cup of apple juice and tried to remember how hot the temperature would be in Louisiana in July. Alice and Gayle would have to be patient with me running beside them in the heat. I was certain to be the slow one, like the slugs that attacked Mom's garden each summer. Sluggish. I giggled to myself. It took me fifteen years to get that saying.

The flight attendant came around for the trash, and I dropped my cup into her bag.

The edge of my ASL book poked out of my tote, the book's cover worn from use. As I'd thought when I first opened David's gift a month ago, it had been the perfect gift for my trip. I only hoped one day I'd be able to tell David in person how much the book had meant to me and helped me. Now that I'd gained a working knowledge of ASL, I'd keep my eyes open for any deaf persons who might need help communicating in the hearing world. After all, time had proven again and again that I was drawn to individuals who didn't easily fit in. Because I once didn't. Neither did Dev. Or my stepsister, Alice.

Enough thinking. I rubbed my temples and then my eyes. Sleep called to me. I tilted the back of my seat just enough to relax and rest my head, with my cardigan rolled and placed to support my neck.

I fell asleep quickly and awoke with a start. A stress dream had jumbled my dogs, Belle and Chanceaux, with

184

the wolf pups grown up, and I had to keep them separated. Dev came to live with us, but she and Alice didn't get along.

The life I was returning to had to be less stressful than that.

When the plane landed, my phone sounded as soon as I turned it on.

Alice: CAN'T WAIT TO SEE U! I MISSED U SO MUCH!

Me: ME TOO!!!

Alice: BE SURE TO FOLLOW THE SIGNS.

Me: DUH!

Alice: ☺ YOU'LL SEE.

It wasn't like Alice to be cryptic. No use wasting time or mental energy trying to figure anything out. I'd find out what she meant in a short while.

As soon as I exited onto the jet bridge, the humidity of south Louisiana slammed me. I broke into a sweat and couldn't wait to get to the air-conditioned terminal.

I kept an eye out for the nearest restroom. My legs wobbled as I hurried through the gate area. Was it just hard to get my land legs back after the long flight, or was I not ready to return to my real life?

Maybe not as ready as I thought. Especially for the possibility of running into David during the rest of the summer. Or definitely at school. And seeing the looks on teachers' faces and hearing whispers about the trouble I'd been in at the end of last semester. I didn't look forward to any of that.

Leaving the restroom, I took a deep breath. I did look forward to seeing my family, but somehow, I suspected the life I'd left behind forty days earlier would've been different had I stayed.

No one waited for me outside the security area. Was the family running late? They would probably catch up with me downstairs in baggage claim.

On legs that worked normally again, I reached the baggage claim area and sought my flight's carousel. White signs bounced up and down above the crowd ahead as families, friends, and drivers tried to attract the attention of loved ones or fares. I returned to my carousel search until I spotted Papa D's head towering above the rest of the crowd. Next to him were Mom and Alice. And, oh my goodness, Jennifer. Then my cousin Jerome, grinning like an alligator, came into view behind Alice.

The sign just behind them and seeming to grow out of Papa D's neck read *WENDY* at the top in bold red letters. Beneath my name was a jumble of capital letters, starting with *BF*. Oh, it was so like Jerome to do something like remind me of my hated nickname, Bird Face. I'd get him for that. But wait a minute… I never told him that nickname.

Grinning and dodging anyone who got in my way, I

continued toward my people. Jennifer stood in front of the group. Their faces sharpened, and I could've counted the freckles on Jennifer's nose.

And... were those David's parents? What were they doing here? Were they with my family?

As I stood blinking and trying to make sense of their presence, David stepped out from behind the others, holding the *WENDY* sign with one hand by a narrow board. He lowered it and smiled that smile I loved so much.

My family and his remained quiet, waiting.

"Hi, Wendy. Welcome home," he said.

Then my family and Jennifer ran up to me, hugging and kissing me and saying how happy they were to see me.

"You look older." Mom held me by the shoulders and studied my face.

"I am older." I laughed.

"You look outdoorsy. Doesn't she, Jerome?" Alice squeezed my arm.

"Like a real Cajun. Welcome home, cuz."

Jennifer pressed her forehead to mine. "I've missed you. Like, forever."

"Me too." I caught a whiff of her hair, still the fragrance of spring.

David stood by quietly, holding the sign close to his side.

When our group settled down so I could turn my

attention to David, I cocked my head and eyed him at an angle. "Did you call me Bird Face on that sign?"

He blushed almost as red as the letters. "No. Of course not. The marker was drying up, and I knew it wouldn't last to spell out what I wanted. So, I used initials. *B, F, W, Y, G, O, W, M.*" He pointed to them as he read them.

"Well, what do they stand for?"

He blushed. "Best Friend, would you go out with me?"

I waited a sec to read his eyes, to see what their expression would be if I didn't answer right away. They morphed from hopeful to scared to hopeful again.

"I will." I wrapped my arms around his shoulders and leaned my head against his chest. His heart thumped its familiar rhythm.

"Are you glad to be home in Louisiana?" His hand rested on the back of my head.

I lifted my face to his. "I am glad. Very glad." I hugged him tighter, and my silver charms jangled on my bracelet like music.

Louisiana was home, but Alaska had become a part of me too.

And it was one thing I could never forget.

Cynthia T. Toney

The Bird Face Series

8 Notes to a Nobody

10 Dates to Girlfriend Status

6 Dates to Disaster

3 Things to Forget

About the Author

Cynthia writes for tweens and teens to show them how wonderful, powerful, and valuable God made them. Her character Wendy and the other teens of the Bird Face series face problems Cynthia too often has seen affecting young people during her life. Cynthia's interests are American Sign Language, Cajun and Italian culture, growing herbs, and rescuing dogs, and those interests are often reflected in her novels. She studies the complex history of the friendly southern U.S. from Georgia to Texas, where she resides with her husband and dogs.

Acknowledgements

This fourth novel of the Bird Face series needed a title containing a numeral, a title that would slip through the lips just as well as the previous ones did. Thank you, Lisa Gefrides, for entering my contest and contributing the winning title for this novel. You clever lady!

Thank you to my friends who, having a lot more knowledge of Jewish culture and practices than I, shared that information with me to bring to life the new characters of Levi and Devorah.

I am grateful to bloggers and other authors who published information about handling deaf characters and who wrote and published stories about young deaf characters. They are too numerous to mention here, but reading about a variety of their methods and treatments proved very helpful. And special thanks to Lill Kohler for her invaluable editing help with this project.

Thanks to all my critique partners who contributed their expertise while I wrote this story, especially Beth, Linda, and Tim.

From the Author

Dear readers:

We have reached the end of the Bird Face series! I wanted to give Wendy a good foundation in these books and then turn her loose to find her own way and become the young woman she wants to be. Perhaps someday I will pick up Wendy's story again after she is grown up.

It was only fitting that Wendy should spend this final story of the series in a state that she could love as much as she does Louisiana. My one visit to Alaska in the mid-nineties impressed me so much that, decades later, I wanted it to be a setting for one of the Bird Face novels.

Although I enjoyed Anchorage and some of the places near it, I was not able to visit the Alaska Wildlife Conservation Center. My husband said we passed right by it on our way to another sightseeing adventure with our family group. I wish I'd known about the center at that time, because I would have insisted on visiting it.

I've taken a few liberties in my story regarding the volunteer program at Alaska Wildlife Conservation Center. Typically, volunteers are at least sixteen years old and take orientation in the spring before volunteering for the following summer. My character Sam and his Alaskan friends are sixteen or older, but my main character, Wendy, turns fifteen shortly after arriving in Alaska.

In the story, Wendy is allowed to be a short-term volunteer because of her circumstances of travelling so far and staying for such a short period of time in Alaska. She takes orientation after she arrives, and she is given easy tasks to do that someone her age can handle. Sam continues to volunteer after she leaves.

A community of Jewish Alaskans exists, and they really do refer to themselves as the Frozen Chosen. I hope that I portrayed my Jewish characters lovingly, as I became very fond of them.

If you have the opportunity to visit Alaska, or if you live there, please take the opportunity to visit the Alaska Wildlife Conservation Center. If you are interested in volunteering, find out more about it at: https://www.alaskawildlife.org/volunteers/

Thank you for reading the Bird Face series, or any part of it you chose to, and for caring about Wendy and her friends as I do.

Gratefully,
Cynthia T. Toney

Discussion Questions

1. What is the capital of Alaska? Where is it located?
2. What is the total square mileage of Alaska? Compare that to Wendy's home state of Louisiana and to your own state. What are the differences in square miles?
3. When did Alaska become a state? How did the U.S. acquire Alaska? Which country separates Alaska from the "lower 48" states?
4. Which common Alaskan animal (air, land, or water) mentioned in the story is your favorite? Why? Which part of Alaska is it most common to? How much does an adult typically weigh?
5. Which thing that Wendy wanted to forget would be the hardest for you to forget? Why? Have you had a similar experience that you'd like to forget? What was it?
6. Fingerspell your first name using American Sign Language. Draw your first name using a drawing of a hand for each ASL letter in your name.
7. Have you ever travelled from home alone and spent more than a day in a place you'd never been before? Did you know anyone there? What did you do to handle loneliness or to meet new people and get along with them?
8. Have you ever tried to maintain a long-distance relationship—friendship or romance? What steps did you take to do so? How long were you successful?

Other YA from Write Integrity

The Award-Winning Rogue Series by Kristen Hogrefe, a dystopian series full of action, romance, and hope!

The Aletheian Journeys is a new fantasy series debuting in early 2019. Those enjoying CS Lewis and JRR Tolkien will love these books!

**Thank you
for reading our books!**

**Look for other books
published by**

Write Integrity Press
www.WriteIntegrity.com

Made in the USA
Middletown, DE
20 July 2020